This is a work of fiction. The events and characters are fictitious. Any similarity to actual people and events are purely coincidental.

"World" Killer

By
A. Antonio

Edited by
Kat Jensen

Night

Eric Highland jolted awake. No matter how many different ringtones he tried, none of them made getting woken up in the middle of the night any easier. He picked up his iPhone to confirm what he expected: his partner was calling.

One of the worst things about being a homicide detective is the phone ringing in the middle of the night. Chances are, it isn't a friend drunk dialing, or even a wrong number. When the phone rang in the middle of the night, it meant someone had died.

Eric swiped his thumb across the screen and groggily answered, "Hey Jose. Where's the body this time? Oh, wait don't tell me ... Paramore again?"

It made sense after all. Paramore is the section of Orlando that you don't drive through once the sun goes down. During the day it isn't all that bad, but the criminals come out as the night wears on. In the last month, three bodies had turned up there. All three had turned out to be drug related murders.

"I wish it was Paramore," replied Sergeant Jose Ortega.

There was something in the tone of Jose's voice that drove the grogginess out of Eric's mind and put him on edge.

Eric had worked with Jose in the Orange County Sheriff's Department for five years now. They had worked countless homicides in that time. From domestic violence to gang related murders, nothing seemed to faze Jose.

What Jose said next left Eric speechless.

"Eric, it's the Polynesian."

Eric tried to process that, but his brain refused. He tried to think of what that could mean, but he already knew. There was only one "Polynesian." The one at Disney World.

The implications of a murder at Disney World were hard to comprehend. Disney World wasn't a place you expected to find any violence. In fact, no murder had ever been committed there.

Over the years, there had been deaths at Disney World, but even those were extremely rare. The fact that over 17 million people a year travel to Disney World and less than one of them dies there, is amazing.

Of course, there are accidents from time to time. Just a couple of years back there had been a monorail accident that claimed the life of one of the employees. There was also a tragic accident where a child was hit by a bus, but never a murder. From time to time, someone died of natural causes, but those didn't "officially" happen on Disney property.

He realized he had said nothing when Jose asked "Eric, you still there?"

"Yeah, sorry. I was just trying to process that," Eric replied.

What Jose said next made everything ten times worse. "Well, there is more. It's a kid. I just wanted you to know in advance."

After five years of some of the most brutal crime scenes that even Hollywood writers couldn't imagine, nothing bothered Eric; nothing except a murdered child.

He had a hard time explaining why the death of a child bothered him so much. When he boiled it down, he figured it was the innocence factor. Adults were rarely innocent; kids, however, were only as bad as their parents. They hadn't had a chance to be bad yet. The kids that people say are bad often have parents who should have been sterilized. Under different tutelage, almost all of those kids would have turned out different.

"Okay, thanks for the heads up. It might take me a little bit to get there. I'll have to use the GPS," Eric replied, as he swung his legs over the side of the bed.

"You're kidding me, right? You've lived in Orlando for over five years and have never been to Disney World?" Jose asked as he started to laugh.

"No, I haven't. I bet there are a lot of people in the Orlando area who haven't been to Disney World," he spat back.

He never had a reason to go to Disney World. Wasn't it just another tourist trap, packed full of screaming kids and miserable parents? He also knew he wasn't alone. He'd met a lot of locals who hadn't been there. He figured he knew enough about Disney World. Between WESH and the Orlando Sentinel, Disney World was always in the news for one thing or another.

That thought made him laugh. Disney World was about to be in the news again, and not in a positive way.

"What's so funny?" Jose asked.

"Oh sorry, it's nothing."

"Hey, before you go! Don't forget, it's your turn to bring the coffee."

Jose didn't get drunk, he didn't smoke, he didn't do drugs, but he was an addict nonetheless. Eric couldn't remember a time when Jose didn't have coffee within reach. He figured Jose must toss back at least two pots a day. The amazing thing was, Jose didn't just drink normal coffee.

"Black with two turbo shots, right?" Eric prodded.

"Has it changed in the last five years, rookie?" replied Jose.

Over the last five years, they had learned how to annoy each other, and they used that knowledge on a regular basis. It was always lighthearted, and it was a good way for them to break the tension that came with a crime scene.

The banter was almost always the same - Eric would ask simple questions that he already knew the answers to; Jose would answer them for a while, until he caught on that Eric was just busting his chops. Then Jose would get annoyed and call him "Rookie" for the rest of the day. In response, he would call Jose "Sarge" and use military terminology, which drove the man nuts.

Jose had spent eight years in the Marines and hated every minute of it Some people thrived under the structure and regimen; not Jose. That fact gave Eric plenty of fodder to work with.

"I'll see you at the location of the murder, Sergeant Ortega, sir!" he barked out.

"Goddamn it! It's way too early ... late ... whatever, for that crap," Jose spat out as he hung up the phone.

He put his phone down on his nightstand and stood up. He stretched his 5'8" frame and rubbed the last of the sleepiness from his eyes.

He looked at the clock at his nightstand. Quarter to 12. He was so out of it when he answered the phone that he hadn't noted the time.

He walked to the bathroom in his compact, one-bedroom house and flicked the light on. He looked at himself briefly in the mirror. His 27-year-old cobalt blue eyes looked back at him. People often thought he wore contact lenses, but his stunning eyes had been passed down from his father and his Scottish Highlands heritage.

Eric had a five o'clock shadow, but he didn't care. You didn't need to look good for a crime scene. Anyways, that's why he kept his dark hair short. He kept it buzzed down to less than a quarter of an inch. It allowed for a clean look even if he didn't have a chance to shower.

Some people thought he cut his own hair because it was so short, but he wasn't that cheap. You could always tell when a guy cut his own hair. There was a reason why you had someone else do it for you. It was something called *quality*. His sideburns were even, his neckline nice and clean and his hair was an even length. When someone cut their own hair, they could rarely claim any of those things, never mind all three.

He grabbed his toothbrush and scrubbed away. The odd thing was, he often did his best thinking while doing menial tasks like brushing his teeth. For some reason, while doing something mindless, his brain tended to put the pieces together. He just hoped that by the end of the day he'd have some pieces to put together.

Teeth clean, he walked back into the bedroom and got dressed. As a detective, he didn't have to wear a uniform. He thanked God for that. Going to a crime scene was bad enough, at least he could be comfortable while he was there.

He pulled on a pair of well-fitting carpenter blue jeans and pulled a black t-shirt over his head. The guys often made fun of him for dressing like this, but that's because he looked good. Most of the other detectives were so out of shape, they looked like slobs wearing a t-shirt.

Eric was in shape. Not the gross body builder "in-shape" but more in the way of a swimmer's body. His muscles weren't huge but they were defined. Because of that, he could get away with wearing a t-shirt and look better than someone in a shirt and tie. That also made him a target for ridicule.

The exception was Jose - six feet of Mexican power, Jose wasn't a bodybuilder, but he was one of the strongest guys Eric knew. It wasn't just useless strength, either. The man once tried out for American Ninja Warrior and would have made it to the finals if he hadn't injured his ankle.

Eric had been blown away when he went to cheer on Jose as he blasted through that ridiculous obstacle course. Jose had done things that day that a human should not be able to do. It should be impossible to run up a wall that bends back toward you, grab the top lip, and then lift your body up over the edge. They called it the warped wall. Only five guys made it over that day. Jose was the only one to do it on his first try.

With a body like that, Jose could easily dress any way he wanted and still look good, but he didn't. When Eric showed up at a crime scene, he often found Jose dressed like something out of the 1950s. Typically, the man wore a shirt and tie, chinos, nice shoes, an overcoat, and a stylish hat. It almost seemed comical.

At first Eric wondered why Jose dressed like a cliched, TV crime drama detective for a crime scene, but he quickly figured it out. People didn't mess with Jose. When he said something, people responded. Even the media was cowed by Jose. It didn't take him long to figure out that Jose's manner of dress added greatly to the power that his partner radiated.

He finished dressing and pulled on his Dr. Marten boots. They added about two inches to his height. He really could care less about how tall he was. He never considered himself to be short, and even if he was, it didn't bother him, but he found that when you could look someone in the eye, or even down at them, it gave you a slight psychological advantage when asking questions. Conversely, when he had to look up at someone it could be a double-edged sword. Sometimes, they assumed he'd try to compensate for being shorter. Other times, they assume an air of superiority. In his line of work, it was better to avoid the issue and be the one to look down.

To The World

Eric walked out the front door of his West New Hampshire Street home and got into his Volkswagen Golf TDI.

A lot of people liked to think they were being "green" by buying a hybrid car. They loved to rave about the gas mileage they were getting as if owning a hybrid car conferred sainthood upon them. The fact was, his five-year-old TDI got better gas mileage than most hybrids. On a bad day, he could get up to 50mpg out of that little diesel monster under the hood, and he didn't have to worry about replacing a massive battery.

That was one thing the hybrid sellers never told their customers. When you hit 100,000 miles, and sometimes less, you had to replace the battery. There went the all the money you saved on gas.

After a stop to pick up two coffees, strong enough to peel paint, he turned onto Princeton Street and then Route 4 south. After a few minutes he got off the highway and turned onto Epcot Center Drive.

He was now in an area he'd never been. Being in the Orange County Sheriff's Department took him all over the Orlando area, but never here.

He soon passed under a large Walt Disney World sign. He also noticed all of the signage changed from the normal green to purple and red. He forgot that he wasn't in Kansas anymore. Disney was its own entity. What they pulled off in the '60s was unprecedented and hadn't been duplicated since. Depending on how the law is read, Disney World is not part of Florida. A lot of concessions were given that no other corporation could ever dream of brokering, even with an army of talented lawyers on their side.

He had to admit, the signs actually had an impact. He could only imagine a family driving down this road and the excitement that must hit them when they saw those signs. They would know they are on vacation.

As he drove down the road, he passed large billboards advertising different rides. He was used to seeing billboards like this. Orlando was full of them. Universal, Sea World, and even Gatorland all had billboards, but something was different about these. He couldn't put his finger on it. He had the feeling that whatever it was would pop into his head the next time he brushed his teeth.

He passed the parking lot for Epcot. He knew he shouldn't have been surprised, but it was huge. The fact that this parking lot surprised him made him laugh a little. From what he'd heard, this wasn't even the biggest parking lot in Disney World.

Continuing down the road, he noticed the Monorail. He was almost disappointed that it was so late, because the Monorail wasn't running. He'd never seen one in action before. He did remember hearing that it cost some insane amount of money to build. It was something foolish like a million dollars a mile, and that was back in the early '70s. He couldn't even fathom how much it would cost now.

He merged onto World Drive. As he drove down the road, it seemed like he was following the monorail. For a moment, that surprised him, until he realized that he had no idea where the Monorail actually went. He had such a flimsy knowledge of Disney World. The scope of his knowledge consisted of what made the news. He knew the monorail cost a million a mile to build, but he couldn't tell you anything else about it to save his life.

He continued down the road and came to something he didn't expect. A large tollbooth was quickly coming up. He followed the signs and got into the right lane. As he did, he counted off the lanes. There were ten lanes just for the Magic Kingdom. How was that possible? Why would you need so many lanes? He made a mental note to ask someone about that.

He turned onto Seven Seas Drive and shook his head. To his right was the Ticket and Transportation Center. Across the street was possibly the largest parking lot he'd ever seen. How on Earth did they secure a parking lot of that size? It seemed like it would be a field day for thieves.

He turned right onto Floridian Way, and his destination appeared before him. The Polynesian Resort in all its glory, stood there in the dark of night.

He pulled in, parked his car, and took in the sight for a moment. He'd seen themed hotels before, but nothing like this one. Somehow they always seemed, well … cheesy. What stood before him was nothing like that. He hadn't even left the parking lot, and it already seemed like he'd been transported out of Florida.

He tried to figure out what it was that was so effective in impressing that feeling upon him. It took a minute, but then it hit him. It wasn't one thing, it was everything. The plants, the architecture, the use of water, and the colors. For a moment he even though the smell was different, but he just shook his head at that idea. There was no way they were pumping a fragrance into the air. At least he didn't think so.

His train of thought was broken when an obviously nervous kid of about 18 approached him. He was wearing a colorful Hawaiian shirt and khakis. On his shirt was a white name tag with blue lettering that proclaimed, "Buddy" with "LSU" under it. Above the name was a picture of some castle. Below the "LSU" it said "Where Dreams Come True." Eric had to laugh at that statement, considering the context of his visit.

"Are you Officer Highland?" asked the employee in a slight southern drawl.

"Yes and no. I'm a detective. I don't care when people get it wrong, but some people will really give you crap for it," Eric replied. Sadly, it was very true. Some people were so obsessed with their title that they would lambast anyone who got it wrong. Eric couldn't care less, as long as the person was polite.

The kid was so nervous he didn't even look up when he said, "I'm supposed to take you to the crime scene."

The "Poly"

As they walked toward the entrance, Eric tried to calm Buddy by making small talk.

"So, you go to LSU? Isn't that a little far to be working at Disney World?"

Buddy stopped as if he was incapable of walking and talking at the same time.

"What? Oh, no, I'm in the College Program. We take a semester or two off and work at Disney World. It's fun and it looks good on a resume when you're done." Buddy explained.

"Do you get credit for it?"

"No, but we get paid. It's not much, but it's enough to break even. It's more about meeting new people and working for the mouse!"

Now he was intrigued. He couldn't help himself, he just had to ask, "I assume by "mouse" you mean Disney. What is so great about that?"

Buddy looked at him like he had just grown a second head. "It's Disney!"

He let it drop. It almost seemed like the kid was on something. He assumed that Disney didn't do drug testing. He couldn't imagine how a kid could be so obsessed about a borderline internship without the help of drugs.

Buddy led him in through the front door to the reception lobby. He stopped dead in his tracks and exclaimed, "What is that!?!"

To call what was in front of him a fountain would be an astonishing understatement. If a fountain was a lemon, than this was the tree. Housed in a two-story atrium, it spanned a solid twenty feet across in both width and depth. It stood well over ten feet high. There was water cascading down from the top.

What really shocked him was the fact that it looked like the building was built around the fountain. More plants than he could count seemed to be growing all over the place. They looked real, too. They didn't appear to be the cheap plastic plants you'd find in many hotel lobbies. The detail they had built into this tiny section of the hotel was incredible.

"They call it the entry or lobby fountain, but the cast members call it the 'Fountain of Youth' because of the feeling people get when they see it," explained Buddy.

"Okay, two questions, first what is a 'cast member' and second, why would anyone put this in a lobby?" he asked as he turned to look at Buddy.

"A cast member is a Disney employee. I don't care when people get it wrong but some people will really give you crap for it," Buddy replied with a big smile spreading across his face. "And the answer to your second question is simple, Welcome to Disney World."

He laughed, slapped Buddy on the back, and said, "You're all right, Buddy."

As they continued through the lobby, his wonder continued to grow. Everywhere, there was vegetation and dark wood accents that made the building feel like someone picked it up from the South Pacific and dropped it in central Florida.

One odd thing occurred to him. So far, he hadn't seen a single room or hallway that would lead to guest rooms.

He called out to Buddy, "Are there any rooms off of the lobby?"

"No. We don't have a lobby. This is the 'Great Ceremonial House.' There are no guest rooms here. We have a place where we check-in guests, numerous dining locations and shops, but no guest rooms."

Buddy then stopped and said, "I'm sorry if that came across as snarky."

He responded, "Don't be. Keep it up. I need to know what things are called and any lingo you use here. You never know what could come in handy later."

"Is there anything else you can tell me about the resort's layout?"

Buddy responded, "Yes. I'll get you a map. All of the buildings are named after places in the Pacific, like Hawaii, Samoa, and Tonga. We are headed to Tokelau."

Buddy went and grabbed a map. When he came back he said something that shocked Eric.

"This has to be the second most notorious thing to ever happen at the Polynesian."

He looked at Buddy sharply and said, "What could possibly be more notorious than a murdered child?"

Buddy staggered a little and sheepishly said "I didn't mean it like that, but ten years from now who is going to talk about a murder? On the other hand, people still talk about the breakup of the Beatles. Anyways, I didn't mean anything by that. I just talk too much when I'm nervous."

Eric looked at him wide eyed and asked, "What are you talking about? The Beatles came here to break up?"

Buddy replied, "No, not all of them. John Lennon was the last member of the Beatles to sign the paperwork to break up the band. He was staying here at the time. They delivered the paperwork to the resort, and he signed the documents while he was here."

Eric smiled at the dorky kid. In some odd way, that made him feel a little better.

As they walked down the lushly decorated path to the Tokelau building, he reviewed the map Buddy had given him. It put a pit in his stomach. There were more than a dozen buildings, a boat launch, a walkway to the *Ticket and Transportation Center* and worst of all, multiple ways to get everywhere. When dealing with a crime scene, you prayed for bottlenecks; anywhere that the killer was forced to go through, to get away. It looked like those were going to be hard come by at the Polynesian.

He hoped this was a crime of passion. If this was planned, it was going to be very difficult to reconstruct what had happened, in a place this large.

Tokelau 3932

Jose Ortega frowned as he looked down at the body. Before him was an African American male, ten to twelve years old. He was flat on his back, in a pool of his own blood. His dead eyes stared at the ceiling and his mouth was slightly open. He was dressed like a typical kid on vacation: cargo shorts and a Mickey Mouse t-shirt. A few feet away was a set of Mickey Mouse ears that had apparently slipped off his head as he fell. Other than where his throat had been slashed open, he looked like your average kid on vacation.

That's what made him frown. The kid's throat was cut. Crimes of passion were grizzly. Multiple stab wounds, bullet holes, or deformed parts of the body where someone had smashed them to a pulp.

This was no crime of passion. Cutting someone's throat took planning. It was a cold, calculated way to kill someone.

There were a number of other things that bothered him about the crime scene. One thing he could not explain was the location of the body. Why was the kid in front of the door? He couldn't quite piece together what had happened, but he knew Eric would.

Eric could be a real pain in the ass, but he was a good guy, if you got to know him. He found great enjoyment in annoying Jose whenever he could. Then again, Jose gave it right back.

When he thought about it, he knew that they made a great team. Influencing people was his specialty. When it came to people, he had a knack for picking them apart. In reality, there wasn't much to it. All he had to do was read the body language, tone of voice, and even the energy coming off a person. Some people had a hard time doing that, but he'd always found it easy, as if he were born with a natural ability that other people lacked.

Eric, on the other hand, was quite different. He wasn't sure if he'd give up his ability with people for Eric's gifts. Eric had the ability to recreate a crime scene. No, it went beyond that. Eric could live a crime. The man had an ability to pick up on the smallest details that other people missed. Sometimes it bordered on uncanny. It almost seemed like Eric's eyes were a video recorder and his brain was a computer. Sometimes it took a while to process, but the man somehow put it all together.

Though he hated to admit it, the best way to explain how well they complimented each other was to recall his military days.

When he was in the Marines, he was deployed to Iraq. Although it wasn't a normal role, one of the guys in Jose's unit adopted a true support role when they came under fire.

They called him "Speedy." His real name was Jake, but like many in the corps, he earned his nickname. When Speedy was around, Jose never had to worry about running out of ammo.

When the bullets flew and you were about to run out, Speedy just seemed to appear next to you with a clip. You often defended yourself with Speedy's bullets.

That was the relationship Eric and Jose shared. Eric seemed to pull the details out of his butt, and he nailed the perps to the wall with them.

"Here come Rookie!" exclaimed El Guapo.

He looked over at El Guapo and smiled. He always smiled when El Guapo butchered the English language. He didn't mean to; he just couldn't help it.

In some ways he felt bad for the man. El Guapo's real name was Fidel Hernandez. He was born and bred in Cuba. His parents had fled the country back in the early '80s and did everything they could to give him what they lacked in Cuba.

El Guapo didn't take that for granted, either. He did everything he could to make his parents proud. He worked harder than anyone Jose knew. When he came to America he didn't speak a word of English. For a young child, to learn English was one thing. For a 16 year old trying to support his parents, learning English was a true task.

He had to admit the man had done well.

He always laughed at the nickname El Guapo. Eric had given it to Fidel and to be honest, Eric was the only one who really got the joke.

Eric gave Fidel that nickname the first time they had met. "El Guapo" meant "the handsome one" when you translated it. Fidel really wasn't that handsome. Instead, Eric gave Fidel that name because he looked just like some relief pitcher the Boston Red Sox had a few years back named Rich Garces.

He was a big baseball fan, but he had never heard of Rich Garces or El Guapo. Eric, however, had sworn that the man was a fan-favorite back in Boston, where Eric had grown up.

He turned around to see Eric walk through the door. For a moment he breathed a sigh of relief when he realized that he was between the body and Eric. Most murders didn't bother Eric, but he knew that kids were another matter.

"Here's your coffee," Eric said as he handed him his extra-large, extra strong, coffee.

"No dairy, right?" Jose asked.

"Of course not. With all those expresso shots you put in there, I bet if you tried to put milk in there too the coffee would kick its butt out of the cup," Eric said with one of his classic smiles.

Jose smiled and then said seriously, "Are you ready for this one?"

The smile dropped off of Eric's face and he just nodded.

He stepped aside and let Eric see the full horror of the scene.

At first, the blood drained from Eric's face, and he looked like he was going to cry or pass out, but then it happened. He'd seen this many times before. There came a point when he could see Eric's brain move beyond the horror and start processing the details.

He could tell that Eric compensated for what he had to look at by detaching himself and turning the crime scene into a puzzle.

Everyone had their own method of coping. Jose's was revenge. He was able to deal with the scene because he channeled it into motivation, a desire to find the animal and see that they were punished. Until he could find the perp, he took out his frustrations in the gym. Whether it was the treadmill or by hitting the weights, Jose found that it was better than anything else for relieving stress.

By the time he had finished his thought, Eric was kicking into action.

"The killer was standing in front of the victim when he killed him," Eric blurted out.

Jose was taken aback and almost asked how Eric knew that, when Eric explained.

"When you cut a major artery, blood tends to spray out at a surprising distance. Notice that there is no blood on or near the door. The killer's body blocked the spray."

He looked at the door and the floor in front of it and just smiled. Eric was right.

"This is weird. The body wasn't moved, but it's close to the door. Why would a kid be close to the door? Where were the parents?" Eric asked as he looked over to him.

"Hold on a sec Rookie, let me fill in what I know before your brain burns out," he said while giving Eric his most disarming smile.

"From what we could get out of the parents, they left the room around 10 p.m. to refill their soda mugs at the restaurant in the rear of the main lobby."

Before he could continue, Eric cut in and said, "Oh, you mean Captain Cook's Snack Co. at the rear of the Great Ceremonial House."

He was dumbfounded for a minute, but then replied while shaking his head, "I know you've never been to Disney World before, so I'm not even going to ask how you know that. Anyway, the parents were only gone for about 15 minutes."

Eric scrunched his brow asked, "Why did they leave the kid behind?"

Jose shrugged and said, "He was watching something on the TV. All I could get out of the parents was that he was watching Stacey. I don't have a clue what that is, but apparently Javon loved it."

He regretted the words as soon as he said them. He'd used the kid's name. He could see Eric wince and he knew it just became that much more real.

It was one thing to see a body and try to figure out what happened, but when it wasn't a body, but a person in front of you, it became very real.

He figured it was just better to continue. "They figured it was Disney World and they were only going to be gone for a few minutes, what could possibly happen?"

He could see Eric start to look all around the room, soaking in all the details.

"You do that thing you do, Rookie?" asked Fidel

He smiled as he saw Eric look over to Fidel and call out "Hey, El Guapo! What's going on?"

Eric then nodded and said, "Yes, I'm going to do it."

Day

When Eric walked out of the front door of the Polynesian, the sun was starting to come up. He felt better now that they were away from the crime scene.

"Are you feeling ok?" Jose asked.

"Yeah, I've got a lot to think about." He then stopped dead in his tracks and asked, "Where are the vultures?!?"

Jose laughed and replied, "This never hit the scanner. Everyone was called in via phone."

His jaw dropped and he said, "Are you kidding me? How did they get away with that?"

Jose just shook his head and explained, "The captain thought it best to keep this one under wraps for as long as possible. After all, this is the first murder in Disney World. The longer the press is out of it, the better. That being said, I got a text from the captain letting me know that it's already on Facebook. You can't move that many people to new rooms in the middle of the night without a few finding out what happened."

Jose looked over at him and said, "We have to interview the parents. After that, I'm going to check out what they're saying on the networks. What do you have going on?"

"I'm going to touch base with our POC at Disney and try to get any info about where the family was during the day. If you come across anything that could help, let me know. I'm also going to Matt and Sally's for dinner later if you need me," Eric said as he looked down at his watch.

"Good. I know when you have time to process this one, you'll knock it out of the park like you normally do," Jose said as he headed for his car.

Eric watched him go for a few seconds before he started for his own car.

He knew that after the interview with the parents he should get some sleep or else Sally would give him hell.

He met Sally when he first moved to Orlando. He walked into her salon and she saw a lonely kid away from home. In twenty minutes, she had pried more out of Eric than anyone else he'd ever known. The next day he was having dinner with her and Matt, her husband.

Eric hadn't often seen the "southern hospitality" you hear about, but Matt and Sally were an ideal example. Even though they were in no way related, they took him in like he was a long lost brother.

On the way to the interview, he placed a call to the person in charge at the Polynesian and explained what kind of information he'd need. He was assured that the information would be securely emailed to him, but they were still in the process of obtaining video footage.

That didn't bother him at all. In fact, it was best if he didn't see any actual footage of the family yet; it was too soon in the process and he didn't want to do anything that could mess up his plan. One of the best things you could do was stick to a plan or checklist. If you did, you were unlikely to miss anything or make any serious mistakes. Most people failed because they got cocky and overconfident. They thought they knew what they were doing. Often they did, until they made a small mistake and the roof caved in.

He was determined that there would be no mistakes with this one. No one was going to kill a kid and walk away, when he was assigned to the case.

The Parents

Jose wasn't thrilled. He'd hoped that once he had the victim's parents in front of him he'd see flaws he could exploit, and in short order have them spilling their guts.

When he looked across the interview table at Mr. and Mrs. Jones, he saw no flaws. Their body language, tone of voice, and manner of speaking all matched someone who had just lost a loved one, not a couple trying to hide something.

He adjusted his voice so it was quieter than normal and added a soft tone to it. His goal was to create a warm, soothing atmosphere. An atmosphere like that tended to calm people and break down any defenses they had put up.

"I want to ask you some questions. Many of them you have already answered, but sometimes when you answer a question a few times, details you missed may come to mind."

The parents just nodded and appeared more than willing to answer the questions he had for them. It was yet another sign that they had nothing to do with the murder. If they were hiding something they would have argued or tensed up.

"How long were you away from the room?"

The father quickly responded, "Only about fifteen minutes. It could have been as long as twenty but we didn't have to wait in line or anything. We just walked over to the soda fountains and back."

He considered stopping the questions. They were giving more info than he asked for and it was information that helped. Guilty people never did that - when they gave additional info they added junk to distract you from the truth.

Before Jose could continue, Eric asked the second question on their list.

"Why did you leave Javon alone in the room?"

The victim's mother started to cry. The father took a breath to steady his nerves before responding, "We were only going to be gone for a few minutes. He was watching TV. We thought he was safe. We have no idea why he opened the door. He knew better."

He looked at Eric and saw he was thinking the same thing. Either the parents had no idea that someone else had opened the door or they were dodging the question. This was an opening that he could use. How the parents reacted to his next statement would speak volumes.

"Javon didn't open the door."

He felt Eric flinch. He knew that Eric had not been expecting him to give away that kind of information in an interview. Typically you never gave information, you only took it. It was a risk, but this time it paid off.

He saw a confused look come over the father that slowly turned into anger. The mother stopped crying. He saw a look of disbelief come over her before she asked, "What do you mean? If someone broke into the room, then why didn't Javon run?"

That was the million-dollar question, and there was only one way he could respond.

"Do you know anyone who lives in the area?"

Both parents just shook their heads.

"Do you have any enemies that knew you were coming down here and where you were staying?"

The father spoke up, "No. We have friends and family back home who knew where we were going, but only our close family knew where we were staying."

Eric asked the next question, "Have either of you been the victim of identity theft?"

Jose nodded at that one. They knew that a wristband assigned to the father had been used to open the room door. If someone had stolen the father's identity, they could have obtained a fake ID, which would have gotten them a new wristband at the front desk. It made no sense that someone would have stolen the father's ID just to kill a kid, but then again, little about this case made sense.

The mother shook her head and said, "No, we signed up for one of those monitoring services. We own a very successful business, we can't risk having our identities stolen."

Jose was getting a little annoyed. They were getting decent information, but nothing that was helping them now. He decided to change the subject.

"Did you notice anyone strange during the day? It could have been at any time during the day."

The father shook his head and started to say no, but the mother grabbed his arm and said, "What about the weird, short guy who was talking to himself?"

The father looked at her and said, "That guy wasn't talking to himself. He was talking into a voice recorder."

Jose didn't think this was going anywhere but he decided to at least inquire about it, "What was he saying?"

The father thought for a minute and said, "It sounded like he was doing a show or something. It had something to do with some kind of Disney Radio. I wasn't paying much attention."

Jose took a big pull on his coffee and then sighed. It looked like they hit another dead end.

After a moment Eric asked, "Did either of you take off your wristbands at any point during the day?"

He had to admit, that was a nicely framed question. If Eric had been more specific he would have led the parents to know the wristbands were involved in a major way. Keeping it vague allowed them some wriggle room.

The father piped up, "No, I don't think either of us did at any point. We didn't want to risk losing them and we wanted to have both of them in case one stopped working. We used them to buy stuff and get into our room. We left all our credit cards and money in the room, so without the bands we would have been locked out and without money."

Jose was done. He knew when it was just a waste of time to keep going. He didn't care that some computer said the father had opened the door. He knew just by looking at the man that he had nothing to do with the murder.

The mother was even less likely. She was barely holding it together. When he looked at her he could almost see the pain radiating off of her.

He looked over at Eric. Eric nodded at him and closed his notepad. It was very unlikely that they would get anything else useful from them.

Home

Eric arrived home and booted up his 17" MacBook Pro. Every time he did, he grimaced. The computer was solid and he never had any issues with it. The problem was, it was now a relic. Apple decided that no one wanted a 17" laptop a few years back so they discontinued them. Apple didn't often make mistakes, but this one seemed like a real dumbass move. He had tried to use a smaller laptop, but quickly went back to his good old workhorse. Once you were used to the larger screen, going back to a 15" wasn't fun.

He opened his email and saw that Disney had already sent him the secure email. He opened the email and noticed something odd. The password-secured attachment was huge. Normally, he received a small text document with an overview of the victim's day. Even then, he often had to stitch together multiple data sources to get an idea of what had happened.

He opened the attachment and was astonished. Inside was more info than he could ever ask for. The information was almost too good. It seemed like someone faked it.

Before his disbelief could wear off, he picked up his iPhone and started to dial his POC at Disney. Before the call could connect, he terminated it. Instead, he called the front desk of the Polynesian. The cast member who answered was more than willing to give him the info he wanted.

He hung up and dialed the number he just obtained.

"Hello," a groggy voice answered.

"Did I wake you up, Buddy?"

"What? Who is this?"

He laughed and responded, "It's Detective Highland."

"Oh, hi. What can I do for you, Detective?"

"I received a bunch of information about the whereabouts of the victim yesterday. Only problem is, it seems impossible that anyone would know this much about where a random kid was during the day. Is there any way they are pulling my chain?" he asked, as he put a slight edge in his voice to try to get Buddy to respond willingly.

After a moment Buddy responded, "No one is pulling your chain. I don't doubt for a minute that we'd have that kind of info. The family was staying on site and was using My Magic Plus. They would have had wristbands with an RFID reader that act as a room key, credit card and park ticket. Beyond that, they can use them to get Fastpasses and trigger interactions in the parks."

He thanked Buddy and hung up.

A big smile crossed his face as he realized he'd just hit the jackpot. It really didn't get much better than this. He'd still get any additional info he could from the parents, like photos, to fill in any blanks he could.

His next call went out to Jose.

When Jose answered he asked "Did you happen to get any photos from the parents?"

Jose laughed and said, "You are not going to believe this. I've got a hell of a lot more than photos for you."

Twenty minutes later, he sat before his computer in total shock. He originally thought the info he got from Disney was the jackpot. As it turned out, he won the lottery twice.

The victim's family had subscribed to a website called TouringPlans.com. The website offered detailed, step-by-step walk-throughs of the parks. The walk-throughs were designed to minimize your time waiting in line. Beyond the itinerary, they were also using the smartphone app the website ran called "Lines." This app allows you to see what other guests are reporting for wait times and it also lets you post any wait times you experienced. The family had used it liberally throughout the day. They not only reported the wait time when they got in line at an attraction, they also posted what they actually experienced for a wait time.

Between the info from Disney, the info from TouringPlans.com, and the family photos, he was going to be able to put together an incredibly detailed "day in the life."

That was his golden technique. It was something he did that made him stand out. He didn't just put together a detailed overview of the victim's last day so they'd have that info as part of the investigation, he put together that information so he could live the last day.

Living the last day of a victim's life gives him the ability to see what others can't. It allows him to pick up on finite details that often turn out to be important.

When he first started trying to live the last day of the victim, his co-workers made fun of him. They soon stopped laughing and sat back in awe. Using his technique, he had blown open his first three murder cases. After that, he revived four cold cases, all of which led to convictions.

His success allowed him to rise to detective at a shockingly young 25. Even today, he was the youngest detective in the department.

He looked again at the data he had in front of him and he smiled. He picked up his phone and sent a text to message Jose that said, "*This bastard doesn't stand a chance!*"

Wildfire

Jose sat back and just looked at his work phone. The Polycom started ringing about an hour ago and it hadn't stopped. He didn't bother to answer, but just let it ring. He knew that soon his voicemail would max out. It was the same old thing he'd been through a number of times before.

Part of it made him sad. When a homeless man was murdered, Jose might get a few calls from the media. When a crime was sensational or someone rich died, his phone virtually exploded, as if that life was worth more than the homeless man. The sad thing was, poor didn't sell.

He leaned back in his chair and shut his eyes. He was bone tired. Not even the coffee was helping, but coffee can only do so much with two hours of sleep.

Just as he was starting to nod off he was startled by someone yelling, "Geesh, Ortega you look like something out of a friggin movie!"

He opened his eyes to see his boss in the door. His name was Captain Reginald Hunter, but despite his gruff manner he preferred to be called Captain or Reggie. The man was a straight shooter. He had no patience for beating around the bush. He told it like it was whether you liked it or not.

Reggie was a good guy, but at the same time couldn't care less if he offended you.

"You're just jealous, Captain," he replied with his best disarming smile.

"Jealous!?! Me!?! I'm not the one dressed to kill. I'm dressed for comfort and performance!" Reggie laughed in his southern drawl.

"You know how it is, Captain. Dressing like this puts the vultures on edge. I'd dress like Lady Gaga if it would shut them up."

A big grin spread across Reggie's face and he said, "Thanks for bringing that up. We need to hold a press conference. Let me rephrase that. *You* need to hold a press conference."

He let out a laugh and sat up, "I knew that one was coming. Don't worry, I'll work my magic."

Two hours later, he stood in front of the vultures. He had expected a large turnout, but this still surprised him. The room wasn't just full; it was packed, and with some unexpected people too.

He had expected the usual crowd from the local papers and TV stations. He had even expected some to make the trip from Tampa. The national correspondents were an unwelcome surprise. New York, D.C., Boston, and more had shown. It almost blew his mind. Those teams must have jumped on a plane as soon as they heard the words "Disney World" and "Murder" mentioned in the same sentence.

He was not one to be intimidated, but he had never been in front of this caliber of a crowd. However, he knew what to do.

Many people think public speaking is just a matter of being comfortable in front of a crowd. In reality, that was only a minor factor. Public speaking could be boiled down to a combination of four things that you could control with practice. The voice is made up three of factors: poise, power and pitch. When those three things were combined with the correct body language, a person can do almost anything with the spoken word.

He adjusted his hat and then took to the podium, stood ramrod straight, slightly narrowed his eyes and tucked his chin just a bit.

Everyone had seen the look before, but few could identify the stance Jose had taken. It was an old Hollywood trick. Villains as far back as anyone could remember often used the same body language. He used it because it was effective. Without even knowing it, the crowd would feel slightly intimidated by looking at him.

He added more volume to his voice while at the same time lowering the pitch. Doing so allowed him to project a booming voice that resonated in the room. This would add to the intimidation.

He proceeded to lay out just the basic details of the murder. He finished by saying that there were no suspects at that time, but they had no reason to feel that the public was in danger.

His efforts to intimidate the crowd worked. Very few questions were raised considering the size of the group before him.

As he stepped down from the podium, he paid a glance toward Reggie, who had a very serious look on his face. As he walked by him, Reggie grabbed him by and arm and said, "Damn, boy, you need to show me how to do that."

Reggie's serious look wasn't one of concern but one of admiration.

Home Cookin'

Eric raised his hand to knock on the Indigo Lake Drive residence. Before his hand had a chance to strike, the door swung open and a jolly looking woman who was almost as round as she was tall greeted him.

"Hey suga, give me a hug and come on in!"

He smiled and gave Sally hug, stepped inside and was overwhelmed with the smell of cooking food.

Sally was round for a reason. She loved to cook. Her husband Matt often said Sally could make anything edible. He claimed she could scrape a flat skunk off the road and make it into a four-star meal.

Sally had never cooked roadkill when they invited him over for dinner. At least if she had, she kept It a secret.

A big, balding, wall of a man appeared in kitchen door.

"Hey Eric, how's it goin," Matt bellowed in his heavy southern drawl.

He often wondered who had the more severe drawl between Sally and Matt. He knew better than to mention it though. When you grew up in Boston, you didn't make fun of other people's accents … unless of course you were in Boston when you did it.

He walked over and shook Matt's ham hock of a hand and then proceeded into the kitchen.

When he saw the table he was thankful. There were only three place settings. Lately, Matt and Sally had decided that they needed to find a girl for him. That had led to some interesting meals. The girls they tried to set him up with were nice, but … southern. He liked southern people, but he often found that he just didn't mesh well with southern girls. He tried dating a few, but it never worked out. He couldn't figure it out. They always ended up having so little in common. In the end, he just figured that it was a cultural thing and some day when he had been fully assimilated into southern lifestyle he'd be able to date someone.

Jose had offered to hook him up with some of the girls he knew. That took him about two whole seconds to decide against. Not only could it have stressed his relationship with Jose, but the kind of girls Jose knew would have eaten him alive. He was a laid back Yankee. Jose often joked around that the Latin girls had the "Spanish Spice" and that it wasn't emotion they showed, it was a lust for life. According to Jose that's why they were the best women on Earth.

When Jose had seen his wide eyes he had laughed and said that maybe someday when he became a real man he he'd hook him up with a real girl.

He looked at the food in front of him. Fried chicken, gravy, mashed potatoes, green beans, and homemade bread covered the table. He loved southern food, but he knew he had to be careful. He wasn't used to eating food with a high fat content, so he had to go easy and not overeat. He had learned that lesson the first time Sally had cooked for him. He spent the next day holding onto the toilet bowl with both hands and praying he didn't blast off.

"Suga, you look tired. Did you sleep last night?" Sally asked with concern on her face.

He looked down and replied, "Not really. I had to work last night."

Seemingly before she even had time to think about it, Sally blurted out, "Oh no did you have to go to that awful child murder on the TV?"

He could only look down. The mention of it forced an image of that poor kid into his head. All he could see was the cold dead eyes staring at nothing. He felt a knot in his stomach and it took everything he had not to cry.

"Ah, shit Sally, why did you have to bring that up!" Matt threw out at his wife.

Faster than the eye could register, Sally's hand flashed out and smacked Matt right across the face. "I will not tolerate that kind of language at my dinner table!"

"Jesus Christ, woman!" Matt bellowed.

Out flashed Sally's hand again to connect with another solid smack to Matt's face. "That includes taking the Lord's name in vain!"

Instead of getting upset Matt broke out laughing. Eric couldn't help himself, he started to laugh too. Sally's face slowly turned red and she spouted out "You think that's funny!?! Well I guess I'll be the only one having dessert tonight!"

Thirty minutes later, he and Matt were sitting in the den trying to tackle huge bowls of peach cobbler. Whenever Sally threatened to hold back food, it was an empty threat. She might as well punish herself. She took great joy in feeding others and seeing them enjoy her food.

When Sally came in and plopped down next to her husband on the sofa, Eric put his bowl down and looked at them. "I need to ask a favor from you guys."

Matt quickly put down his bowl and leaned forward, "What is it? Is everything ok?"

"You know I'm working the murder at the Poly. I've told you guys about that thing I do where I try to relive the last day of the victim's life."

He paused for a minute before continuing, "I wanted to know if you two could act like you were my parents tomorrow. I don't know anyone else I could ask."

"Suga, are you asking us to go to Disney World?" Sally asked.

"Yes. We'd pay you for your time and pay all the expenses …"

Before he could continue, both Sally and Matt jumped up and yelled "Woooo!"

When they calmed down Matt explained, "We love Disney. We can't afford annual passes and the tickets are crazy expensive. This is awesome! We can't wait!"

It took a moment for him to process that. He couldn't quite grasp why they were so enthused. Finally he said, "Great. Pack an overnight bag and meet me at the Poly in two hours."

He was afraid he said something wrong when he saw both Sally's and Matt's mouths fall open.

"We get to stay at the Polynesian Resort?!? HOLY SHIT!!"

He swore he heard the slap before his eyes were able to register the movement of Sally's hand.

"LANGUAGE!"

Tourists

When Eric saw Matt and Sally arrive, it looked like they were floating on air. He didn't think there was anything he could have done to wipe the smiles off of their faces.

Together they walked around the "fountain of youth" to the guest registration.

The way Sally cooed when she got her My Magic Plus bracelet you would have thought someone had just given her a diamond ring. The bracelet wasn't even that attractive; it was different shades of gray.

After they were done checking in and getting everything registered, Sally hustled her hefty frame over to the fountain. Matt was right on her heels with a camera.

Eric couldn't help himself, and he started to laugh at them. He couldn't tell if they were hamming it up and acting like tourists for his benefit, or if they were seriously that excited.

"Eric, come take our picture!" Matt yelled out.

Before he could respond, a cast member walking by stopped and said, "I can do it so all of you can be in the photo."

He watched as Sally's face lit up at the notion. She ran over, grabbed him by the arm and dragged him back to the fountain. He didn't even have to smile when the cast member took the photo because he was laughing too hard.

They didn't stay in 3932 because it was still a crime scene. Instead, they stayed in the room next to it. They were the only ones in the building. All the other guests had been moved.

He approached the door and waved his wrist over the lock. He couldn't suppress a smile as the door unlocked. It really was a cool feature to just wave your hand and see things happen.

He held the door open for Sally. It was a good thing, too. He was quite sure that if hadn't, she would have run him over. Matt followed right on her heels. They were funny to watch. They ran all over the room looking at everything. They even ran into the bathroom, oooed and ahhhhed, ran back out and oooed and ahhhed some more.

Matt ran over to the TV and turned it on. He jolted as he heard a nasally voice start booming out of the TV. He heard Matt exclaim, "Wooo! It's Stacey!"

"Sorry but you have to turn that off. I can't see that yet," Eric quickly explained.

"No problem," Matt said as he changed the channel.

Eric took a minute to look around the room. At the crime scene he had observed things in a very different way. This time he soaked in the details. It quickly became clear that whoever designed the room had spent a lot of time on the little things. The way the carpet, wallpaper, and bedspread offset each other was impressive. The color scheme and decorations all played toward the overall theme of the resort.

He looked at a painting next to one of the beds. It depicted a beach scene at night in what must be the south Pacific. At first it just seemed like a random run-of-the-mill painting you'd find in any hotel room, but then something caught his eye. He noticed three black circles cleverly camouflaged into the painting. He thought it must be some accident or a fluke of his imagination. The human brain had a natural ability called matrixing. In a sense, if your brain could not clearly identify something it had an odd ability to infer that you are looking at something else. It's why you can look at a cloud and see a flying pig or some other shape that isn't really there.

"Looks like a Mickey head," he muttered to himself.

"Oooooooo! Did you find a hidden Mickey!?!" Sally screeched as she and Matt rushed over.

"A what?" he asked.

"A hidden Mickey. The Imagineers hide them in rides and random places. There are websites and books dedicated to logging all of them. Some are much harder to see than others. Like this one. Where do you see it?" Matt asked as he stuck his face so close to the picture he his nose seemed like it was touching it.

He assumed that an "Imagineer" was Disney for research and development. That seemed to fit. What really left him scratching his head was the fact that they put so much effort into a detail that only a minuscule minority would ever pick up on. So far, though that's what he had seen over and over again when it came to this place.

Sally ran over to the sliding glass door that led to the balcony and threw open the curtains. This time he was the one who almost oooed and ahhed. The room looked out onto an open yard with a massive tree in the middle. He just stood there next to Sally for a moment before opening the door and stepping out. He was almost overwhelmed for a moment. During the day this place took on a completely different feel. The sun was starting to go down, casting warm hues over all the vegetation. Music quietly flooded the air, which only enhanced the warm feeling growing inside him.

He hadn't even noticed that Sally had joined him on the balcony.

"It's something else isn't it?" she asked.

All he could do was nod his head in agreement.

"Suga, you really look tired. Maybe you should take a nap," Sally said as she gave him her best motherly look.

He just smirked and explained that he was too worked up.

"I can fix that," bellowed Matt from behind them.

"You're not a kid till tomorrow, right?"

He gave him a puzzled look and said, "Yeah, I start my technique first thing in the morning."

"Then I'd say we have a date with Tambu!" Matt said as a huge grin spread across his plump face.

"I'm almost afraid to ask, but what is a 'Tambu?'" he asked as he looked between Matt and Sally.

Before Matt could open his mouth, Sally put her hands on her hips and said, "It's a place where the devil goes to corrupt foolish men."

"What on Earth are you talking about?" he asked as he glanced nervously at Sally.

"Hey, you're the detective. What kind of place would cause Sally to say that, and me to guarantee that it will help you sleep?" Matt asked as he planted a hand on Eric's shoulder.

Eric thought for a moment and then it occurred to him. "Ah, a bar! Lead the way, my friend!"

Kungaloosh!

Sally just shook her head as Matt and Eric headed out the door.

When they got to the Tambu Lounge, Eric sat on one of the bar stools and looked around. The decor was impeccable. The dark woods and tiki statues really seemed to fit the atmosphere. The stonework on the floor led up to the stonework on the bottom of the bar. Above the square bar there was a thatched roof that sat below the ceiling of the lounge. Away from the bar were floor-to-ceiling windows that looked over the resort.

He really had a hard time believing that anyone would put so much effort into building a bar, but it was obvious that someone spent a lot of time designing this one.

Matt sat down next to him and slapped a ten-dollar bill down on the bar.

"Hey, it's on me man," he started to protest.

Matt held up his hand and quickly explained, "I'm not buying a round; I'm priming the pump."

Before he could ask what that meant, Matt nodded to the cast member who was tending bar as he pushed the bill forward. The cast member deftly slipped the bill into a pocket and asked what they would like.

"I'll have a Jack and Coke," Matt said.

He could hear the excitement in Matt's voice. He knew that Sally did not allow any alcohol in their house. Her father was an alcoholic and he had not been a happy drunk. Whether it was sad or a blessing, he drank himself into an early grave. He knew that Matt was not an alcoholic, but he did like a good drink. It was something he rarely got to enjoy.

"Glenlivet on the rocks," he responded when the bartender turned to him.

The cast member quickly poured their drinks and placed them on napkins in front of them.

His eyes almost bulged out of his head. He didn't think he had to stipulate he wanted a normal pour, not a double, but before he could respond the bartender asked for $14.

As he paid he looked at Matt who smiled and whispered, "Prime the pump."

He put the glass under his nose and took a whiff. There is something about the smell of a good Scotch that is very relaxing. He really enjoyed Glenlivet, or at least some of them. His favorite was the 16 year old. They called it Nadurra. It was a cask strength single malt Scotch. For a 100 proof whiskey, it was exceptionally smooth and had one of the most unique finishes of any Scotch he had ever tried. His second choice was what he was drinking now; the regular Glenlivet. For some reason, he found the 12 year single malt to be better than the 15 and even the 18 year old. He'd only bought the 18 year old once. He was sorely disappointed. For a Scotch that cost almost twice as much as the 12 year, it really wasn't much better.

After he took a big swig of his Jack and Coke, Matt looked over at his drink and asked what it was.

"It's just Scotch and ice," he quietly explained.

"I've never had Scotch. It's just a kind of whisky right?" Matt asked as he looked more closely at Eric's drink.

He pushed the tumbler glass toward his friend so he could take a sip.

Matt picked up the glass and took a big swig. His eyes bulged and he looked like he was going to spit back into the glass. To his credit he forced it down and said, "God that tastes like a horse pissed out a campfire! I couldn't drink that even if it was mixed into something."

"It's good stuff, and you'd never mix one of that quality into a drink," he laughed.

"Bah! If I'm going to drink something straight it's going to be real alcohol; good bourbon like Knob Creek or Bookers. It certainly wouldn't be some swill a bunch of guys wearing skirts threw together," Matt said with a thunderous laugh.

"Jeese Matt, you are such a Philistine," he said smiling.

"Umm … thanks!" Matt said warily.

He could tell that Matt had no idea what a Philistine was, despite the fact he went to church with Sally every Sunday. It always amazed him how little most professed Christians knew about the Bible. He wasn't really a religious guy, but he'd bet good money that he knew more about the Bible than 90% of the "Christians" out there. He once discussed that very thought with Sally. She explained that it was about what was in your heart, not your head. No matter how long he thought about that, he couldn't wrap his head around an idea like that.

In some ways he envied Sally. To be able to trust something so completely and find peace from it based on a feeling was something he could not do. He knew exactly why. Too often in his line of work, your gut feeling failed you. Sometimes you were sure you knew something, only to uncover a fact that shattered everything you believed. If he could ever find a religion that based all of its teachings on something tangible instead of traditions and "feelings" he might be in business.

He drained the rest of his glass. Seeing it was time for round two, Matt slurped down the remaining half of his drink in one gulp.

"I'll have another," Matt cried out and then let loose a weakly muffled belch.

"Would you like another Scotch, sir?" the cast member asked him.

He thought for a minute and then said, "No. I want something Disney."

He wasn't sure that there was such a thing as a Disney drink, but then the cast member smiled and yelled out one word, "Kungaloosh!"

A few people around the bar, including Matt, replied with an emphatic, "Kungaloosh!"

He watched as the cast member mixed one cup of strawberry daiquiri mix, ¼ cup of orange juice, ¼ cup of Captain Morgan's spiced rum, and ¼ cup of blackberry brandy. He took that concoction and threw it in a blender with some ice.

He looked at the drink before him and wasn't sure he even wanted to sip it. It looked sweet enough to send a diabetic into shock. Not only that, it had four ounces of booze in it. The drink was massive.

He hesitantly took a sip. It didn't seem possible, but it worked. It worked quite well. In fact, it was one of those drinks that could be labeled as lethal. In his book any drink that didn't have that alcohol bite as you drank it was lethal.

You could never tell how much you really drank until you tried to stand up.

"It's good shit, right?" asked Matt with a knowing smile.

"Do I have to slap you since Sally's not here?" he asked as a grin broke across his face.

Matt laughed, but he was only half kidding. One thing that got under his skin was profanity. He always viewed it as a sign of ignorance. There were so many words in the English language and so many ways you could say the same thing, there was no excuse to use the same vulgar words over and over. He had met some people who used profanity like other people used commas. It amazed him how some people could function with such a small vocabulary.

In the end, if you frequently used profanity he figured you were one of three things: you were either ignorant, lazy or both.

"Hurry up and suck that thing down. We're going to be late!" Matt exclaimed.

"Late for what?" he asked as he looked up from his drink.

A mischievous look spread across Matt's face and he said, "You'll see."

Pieces

Jose sat behind his cheap Walmart desk in his small home office. He shifted in his chair and rubbed his eyes. No matter what he did, he just could not get comfortable. He actually liked the desk because he found the layout to be very usable. There was no fluff to speak of, and there was very little wasted space. The only problem was, the desk was so cheap it was starting to fall apart. He had actually duct-taped parts of it together. His girlfriend had really teased him about that, but he didn't care, he liked it. What he did care about was his crappy office chair. Every time he sat down he promised himself that he would buy a new one.

Ignoring his discomfort, he leaned forward and frowned as he looked at the first in-depth round of data spread out before him. It would be a while before they got all of the forensics back from the lab and extracted more info from the parents and cast members at the resort. He honestly wondered if they were going to need it.

The door to the room was unlocked by the victim's father. There was little doubt about it. The security system the RFID readers registered who was who. Apparently Disney had set it up that way so various interactions in the park could use the guest's name. It was a nice touch. It was even nicer when trying to figure out a murder.

The victim's mother had used her bracelet to get the

drinks, so she was out as the murderer, but she could be covering for the father, which would put her away for a long time.

They had also figured out what the murder weapon was. The victim's throat was so cleanly cut that their search was narrowed down dramatically. Only two things could cut like that: a surgical scalpel or a straight razor.

The wizards in the lab had the ability to determine how thick the blade was based on the cut itself. They were looking for a straight razor. More specifically they were likely looking for a folding straight razor.

He prayed that the father shaved with a straight razor. If he did, this case would be closed within a couple of days. If he didn't, they'd have to break one of the parents. Considering what they had, that would be hard. In the interview, they seemed like they were totally innocent.

What he now had to distill from evidence was a motive. A good motive could help him crack the parents if he had to. The problem was, he didn't have a motive. He had enough info to choke a goat, but nothing, absolutely nothing, pointed to a motive. Without a motive he knew they would be shooting in the dark. Juries don't care how much evidence you have. If you couldn't tell them why someone killed, your odds of getting a conviction were not good. They normally didn't acquit, but more often than not, you'd end up with a hung jury.

He smiled to himself, though. He knew he had an ace up his sleeve. Eric was doing his walk-through tomorrow. If anyone could figure out the motive, it was Eric. Still, something was nagging at him.

If the parents did it, they were amazingly good actors. He had seen a lot of crocodile tears over the years. He could normally pick up on fake crying within seconds. People who faked crying might be able to force tears out, but their body language was all wrong.

Only once had he been wrong. He remembered that case like it was yesterday. A man had killed his older brother. He was totally convinced that the younger brother was innocent. The guy had done everything right. All his reactions had matched those of an innocent person. Time and again, he interrogated the guy with no changes, not even a slight slip. No one could possibly act that perfectly. Boy, did Eric ever save his ass on that one.

Eric had done his walk-through on the victim. In the process he had figured out a dark secret the family had hidden. The family had a history of multiple personality disorder. Not only had he figured that out, he also found out how to bring out the hidden personality in the younger brother.

In the final interrogation, Eric triggered that hidden personality. The change in the man had been so startling it made the blood drain from his face. Everything seemed to change. He swore the man even looked different.

Ever since that day, he had tried to make no assumptions until everyone on the case agreed. When all eyes saw the same thing from their different angles, it was normally safe to assume you had your answer.

The nagging feeling would not leave him. The body language was not right. What were the odds that the dad and mother both suffered from multiple personality disorder?

The Pageant

The double shot of Scotch and the massive Kungaloosh had Eric feeling quite goofy. He didn't care where Matt was dragging him, knowing he could enjoy almost anything in this state.

He followed Matt down the torch-lit path. He found more often than not, he wasn't even looking where he was going, utterly distracted by his surroundings. What really grabbed his attention was the pool. After everything he'd seen in this place he didn't think anything would surprise him. The pool proved that idea wrong.

It was a fairly large, zero entry pool. That in itself wasn't impressive. Although they were cool, he had seen those before. What really stood out about this pool was the massive steaming volcano attached to it. He could see a water slide that came out of the volcano and dumped into the pool. In his frame of mind, he wanted to tear his clothes off and go for a ride.

Matt led him to a beach on the lake. He just stared across the water. In front of them the expanse of still water stretched off into the dark. Beyond the lake stood a brightly lit castle, which slowly changed colors from blue to purple to pink and so on.

Eric looked around and noticed that there were a number of people on the beach with them. It was a nice view, but not one to draw a crowd and keep them there.

Just then Eric noticed something floating by in the dark. It was too dark to make out what it was. He just stood there staring at it, trying to figure out what it was, when the music started.

The music that assaulted Eric's ears sounded like someone gave a monkey a synthesizer. It was straight out of the '70s. This made it the perfect fit for what appeared floating on the dark water.

Slowly, different images appeared. All of them looked like something a kid made with a Lite-Brite, but slightly animated. Each time a new image appeared, the music would change.

Suddenly, the music stopped, but the images were still there. Eric thought something must have broken when the castle in the background went dark.

At first, the cop inside of Eric kicked in. He thought something was wrong. A pit was starting to form in his stomach. That pit turned to elation when a new sound track started and a starburst erupted above the castle. The lights turned back on as one firework after another lit up the sky.

In front of him, the images from the light show continued to appear and the fireworks in the background reflected off of the still lake. Eric felt a little lightheaded and realized he was so overwhelmed he had forgotten to breathe.

At one point a red octopus appeared directly in front of him as purple fireworks burst in the background. It seemed impossible, but it was as if the light show in front of him was working in concert with the fireworks in the background.

All of a sudden, all the images disappeared and were replaced with American flags and stars. They flashed back and forth and then disappeared. The light show was over but the fireworks continued. After a few more minutes, the music hit a crescendo and the entire sky seemed to fill with fireworks.

After it was over, he just stood there for a moment. He'd never seen a fireworks display like that. Not only were the quality and quantity impressive, but he'd definitely never seen a display that was so perfectly timed to music.

"Did you like that, suga?"

He turned around to see Sally standing there with Matt's arm draped around her shoulders.

"This is the only place I've seen that combo," she

continued. "All the resorts on the lake get to see the Electric Water Pageant and you can see Wishes from some of them, but this is the only one where you can see them both at the same time."

Part of him suddenly felt overwhelmed. Instinctively, he wondered if he was dreaming. He dispelled that idea when he heard Buddy's voice in his head.

"It's Disney World!"

Tonga

Eric's alarm went off and he muttered under his breath. What kind of a person gets up at six in the morning on vacation? He sat up and looked toward the sliding glass door in time to see Sally and Matt step back into the room. They appeared to be fully dressed and ready to go.

He muttered to himself again. This was going to be a long day.

After he showered, he brushed his teeth at one of the dual sinks in the bathroom. It was a large bathroom for a hotel. Everything was high quality too, even the complimentary toiletries.

He suddenly stopped brushing and said quietly to himself, "Whimsy."

His brain had done it again. When he stopped thinking and let his brain take over, it figured out one of the cataloged puzzles stuck in his head.

The day before, he couldn't figure out what it was about the Disney World billboards that incited such an emotional response. At the time he couldn't place it, but now his brain did it for him.

The billboards were whimsical in a way he had never seen anywhere else. He wondered how long Disney had researched billboards to discover that little trick.

He finished brushing his teeth and got dressed. Instead of his normal blue jeans he pulled on a pair of cargo shorts. Next, he pulled on a Mickey Mouse t-shirt and finished the look off with a pair of sneakers, identical to the ones the victim had been wearing.

This was one of the things he did that made people laugh. He tried to recreate everything the victim did. Even the way they dressed, if possible. Granted, he didn't go overboard with it and dress in drag if the victim was female, but he did his best.

Matt banged on the bathroom door and yelled, "Come on man, we're gonna be late!"

He looked down at a cheap Casio digital watch, very similar to the one the victim had been wearing. It was 6:20. They had fifteen minutes to make it over to the Kona Café for their breakfast reservation.

He opened the bathroom door. Both Matt and Sally were waiting for him.

"Hey, looking good, suga. It's nice to see you dressed a little less flashy," Sally said as she smiled up at him.

He stopped and looked at Matt for a moment. He had some odd orange and brown baseball cap on. Across the front of it, it had something written in Spanish. His Spanish wasn't as good as it should have been, but it said something about doors. He started to ask what it meant but he thought better of it.

They walked by room 3932 as they left the building. He couldn't help but wince as they passed. He knew the body was gone and most of the scene had been processed, but he couldn't get the image of it out of his head. It hit him that much harder now that he was walking in the victim's footsteps. Just 48 hours earlier that little boy, Javon, had walked where he was walking. He tried to envision the scene. Tried to think about what Javon had thought and felt.

He thought about last night and the show he'd seen at the beach. He felt an energy building inside of him. If his day even came close to the excitement of last night, he wondered how Javon kept from bouncing off the walls.

Unintentionally, he started walking faster. When Sally called out, "Well, ain't we in a rush," he knew he'd managed to get a grasp on Javon's state of mind.

He took a seat next to Sally when they arrived at the Kona Café. Matt and Sally had started to sit next to each other when he reminded them that parents with a ten year old almost never sat together. One of them always sat next to the child, in case the kid acted up.

He was pleased by the Kona Café. It was more laid back than the rest of the Polynesian, which could be overwhelming at times. Overall, the café had a nice warm feeling to it. The only thing that really stood out were the fans in the ceiling. They were just bizarre. The only way to really describe them was to say someone took hollowed out metal logs and stuck fans in them. The logs would spin. The effect was the blades of the fan spun vertically instead of the normal horizontal.

He pulled out his phone and looked up what he had to order. It was something called Tonga Toast. Toast sounded reasonable for ten-year-old kid and even more so when it looked like he had washed it down with an OJ.

He looked at the menu anyway. He didn't really look at the items or descriptions. Instead, he looked at the colors and layout. He tried to grasp how it would have impacted a child. It was well known that color and shape influenced what people felt. It was also a fact that the best menus were laid out in a very precise manner. It was an art form based on a lot of research. Without knowing it, people always looked at a menu the same way. No one picked up a menu and read it top to bottom, left to right. The most expensive items were always placed where people looked first. That's why you rarely saw a menu laid out by price or alphabetically.

The cast member came over and took their order. He laughed when Matt ordered. He ordered something called "*Big Kahuna*." If there was a more fitting thing for Matt to order he didn't know what it was. He also ordered a pot of

Kona coffee, which made him envious. Kids didn't drink coffee. If any did, he prayed he'd never have to meet them.

He almost bit through his lip so he didn't laugh when Sally ordered. She ordered the fruit plate. Sometimes Sally was a total nut job. Her home cooking consisted of fat, meat, carbs, and more fat. When she was outside the home she ate like a model before a shoot.

When the drinks came, he almost ground his teeth. Matt didn't just get coffee. It was in a French press. From across the table he could smell it. He wondered if any coffee had ever smelled better. All he could do was sit there and sip his OJ.

"Christ, that's good," Matt muttered to himself as he sipped the coffee.

He was out of smacking range so Sally smacked her small, meaty fist on the table and gave him a stare that could have burned through a wall of solid titanium.

Matt just giggled, apologized and tried not to look directly at her.

He sat there and thought about how much of an odd couple Matt and Sally were. For everything they had in common, they had twice as many things that made them opposites. It occurred to Eric that their differences were what made them such a good couple. Sally was like a mother hen who wasn't happy unless she was taking care of someone. Matt was kind of a wreck who'd forget to put pants on before he left the house unless someone reminded him.

There it was. Matt needed Sally and she needed him. In the end it didn't matter if you were opposites, if that was the final summation of your relationship.

When the food came, his eyes nearly popped out of his head. What was laid before him was far from the "toast" he expected. He'd gotten boxes from Amazon.com that were smaller than this thing. He grabbed his phone and punched "Tonga Toast" into Google to find out what he had gotten himself into. He clicked a link for the "Disneyfoodblog.com." He just shook his head when he saw the description.

Banana-stuffed Sourdough French Toast rolled in Cinnamon Sugar and served with Strawberry Compote.

He sat there and wondered what parent on Earth would let a ten year old kid order that? When he looked up and saw an obviously happy Matt diving into what looked like the morbidly obese love child of French Toast and a pineapple, he figured it out: parents on vacation.

Pressure

Jose entered his office to find Reggie waiting for him. He could tell just by looking at the man that he was on edge.

"I got a call from the governor. He wanted to know how the Disney case is going," Reggie said as he paced the small office.

"Captain, it's been less than two days. We don't even have a majority of the forensics back yet," he said, as he took off his hat and hung it on the wall.

"I know, I know. Are we at least making progress?" Reggie inquired with more than a hint of desperation in his voice.

He shifted his weight to one foot, nodded, and smiled, before replying in his smoothest voice: "We've got some great evidence, and a mountain of data. Eric is out as we speak doing one of his walk-throughs. Tomorrow he'll fill in the blanks, and on Thursday we have that meeting with our regular crew and the security expert from Disney. I'm almost certain we'll have a clear idea of what happened."

"Good. That should work," Reggie said, but he kept pacing.

"Anything else, Captain?" Jose asked, as he glanced in Reggie's direction.

"No, no. This case just has me on edge. Murders are bad,

high profile murders are worse, and kids are as bad as it gets. I mean, what kind of sicko kills a kid?" Reggie looked him in the eye before finishing, "Plus, the governor has never called before. If we're not careful, this could get out of control fast."

He watched Reggie leave his office. He took a big pull on his coffee and tried to clear his thoughts. Nervousness had already set in after seeing the first round of evidence. This was not news he wanted to hear. For some reason he still couldn't shake that nagging feeling that something wasn't right. He didn't think anything was faked, but at the same time, it didn't seem like the pieces were fitting like they should. It was almost as if they had the pieces, but couldn't identify the picture they formed.

He booted up his PC to go over the evidence again. Maybe there was something he missed.

He pored over the details they had so far. Nothing was sticking out. It seemed cut-and-dried. Everything was pointing to the father.

He finished his coffee and got up to go get another mug. As he walked over to the coffee maker, he decided that he'd pull as much info on the parents as he could. Maybe there was an insurance policy or something else to point to motive. Maybe he'd get lucky and find something that could help. He just had to be careful. If he put in too many inquires on the parents, someone would catch wind. If that happened, he knew what they were in for. Someone would leak the info to the press. That was the last thing he wanted.

It was bad enough for someone who was innocent to get labeled as a suspect. It was something else entirely to label the parents. You had to be sure if you were going to point the finger at the parents. That was a mistake you did not want to make. The press showed no mercy when it came to those kind of mistakes.

Monorail

When Eric stood up, he could barely walk. He only finished half the Tonga Toast and the bacon that came with it. He felt like he'd need to run for an hour to even start to burn that meal off.

"Who's driving?" he asked as he looked at his friends.

He got the strangest look, so he quickly ran his tongue over his teeth to see if he had anything stuck in them. Then he looked down to see if he had slopped anything on his shirt.

"Suga, ya don't drive when ya stay at the Polynesian," Sally said in a slightly condescending tone.

"Why, is there a bus or something?" he asked as he looked between his friends.

"I'd say it's definitely 'or something,'" Matt said before explaining, "Do you know what they call the Polynesian? It's one of three monorail resorts."

He had seen the monorail tracks and thought they just passed the resort. He hadn't realized that the monorail actually stopped here.

He followed Matt and Sally around the open second floor of the Great Ceremonial House toward the front of the resort.

They passed through some sliding glass doors and stepped out onto a covered walkway. Even though they were on the second floor, on either side of them was lush vegetation. On the right there was a small pool with a waterspout shooting into the air. A small rainbow formed as the morning light passed through the water. Something told him that they designed it that way.

They reached the end of the bridge and walked into the monorail station. It reminded him of a clean, well-organized mass transit station. There were sliding gates, with people lined up behind, which seemed like they would go a long way in reducing the chaos that normally followed the arrival of a train.

He instinctively looked down the track. He always did that at a station. He was used to riding mass transit. When you grew up in Boston you rode the "T" every day. He could see it in his mind's eye now. He could imagine waiting at Government Center and looking down the track. You always heard the "T" before it arrived. The screeching of the wheels and electric hum always floated out of the tunnel before the train came into view.

Without thinking about it, he started to hear "Shipping Up To Boston" in his head. He was a big fan of the Dropkick Murphys. When you grew up surrounded by the hardcore/punk scene of Boston, you typically ended up liking the Dropkicks.

He had liked them well before they became famous. He could still hear the original version of "Barroom Hero" in his head. He liked Al Barr, but Al could not sing that song like Mike McColgan could. It was funny, most people didn't even know Al Barr wasn't the original lead singer. Back then only Mike sang, with Ken Casey chiming in, rarely.

Some of the purists didn't like it when Al Barr joined the band. Eric thought he was a great fit. Al had paid his dues. He had been the lead singer of the Bruisers, a punk/rockabilly/Oi band out of Portsmouth, NH. They had never reached the popularity of the Dropkicks, which had ensured the band members stayed real. Eric remembered meeting Al after a show at the now-defunct Elvis Room in Portsmouth when he was a teenager. Al had been approachable and friendly. It had also amazed him when Al had turned down an opportunity to go drinking with some of the guys after the show. He had explained that he had to work the next day. Eric had asked where he worked, imagining some local music store something edgy. He nearly fell off his chair when Al told him he worked at a local independent grocery store in neighboring Kittery, called "The Golden Harvest."

He wondered if Al would remember him or if he'd even be approachable anymore. He decided it was unlikely. A vast majority of the famous people he had met had been total pricks. He just hoped Al hadn't forgotten his roots.

Startling out of his reverie, he jumped a little as the

monorail train came into view. It made almost no noise as it approached the station. It also didn't look like the trains he was used to. It was more futuristic. Its lines were smoother and down the side of the entire train was a long black stripe.

"Sweet! We get to ride black today," Matt cried out to Sally.

He turned to them and gave them a confused look.

"Matt is a monorail nut. Even though there is no real difference between them, black is his favorite. Each train has a different color stripe down the side of it," Sally explained.

The monorail stopped. The doors opened and they stepped aboard. He was surprised. All of the sections were separated. He wondered why they would do that. You could fit a lot more people if the train was hollow and connected. It finally occurred to him: allowing fewer people on at a time allowed for a much more pleasant ride. He bet that would be very important in the middle of the summer, when people had been sweating in the Florida sun all day. It was bad enough in Boston. He couldn't imagine Florida.

A recorded voice came on over the intercom and said, "Please stand clear of the doors;" "Por favor, manténgase alejado de las puertas."

He started to laugh to himself. He knew what Matt's hat was about now. He was a bigger dork than he thought.

That wasn't fair, though. Everyone had a dorky side. There was that one thing that everyone had that other people would think was dorky. For him it was Moonshiners. He didn't tell people he watched that show. It was one of the few shows he watched religiously. He couldn't explain why. The people were ridiculous. They were all criminals. Between the lot of them, they either didn't wear shirts, were missing teeth or bastardized the English language so badly they had to give them subtitles so people who spoke English could understand them. Despite all that, he couldn't stop watching.

He stopped and wondered which was worse, being a monorail freak, or being a Moonshiners fan. He decided that it was Moonshiners. Matt wasn't afraid to wear his obsession like a badge of honor. He would be mortified if anyone found out he loved Moonshiners.

As they traveled around the lake, they stopped at the Grand Floridian Resort. It reminded Eric of something, but he couldn't place it. It was almost like he'd seen the hotel before, but he shook the feeling off. Having never been to Disney, he'd definitely never been to this resort before.

Something stood out to Eric as they went. All the announcements were prerecorded and easy to understand. He remembered riding the "T" as a kid. The operator announced the stops, and they were often so muffled that there was no way you'd know what stop you were at until you saw the sign in the station. The recorded announcements were much nicer.

He noticed something else that elevated Matt's dorkiness to a new plateau. Right on cue, he was muttering the announcements word for word to himself.

Sally caught him staring at Matt, shrugged her shoulders and explained, "For special occasions we'll go to one of the monorail resorts for dinner. After that, we'll ride the monorail loop a couple of times."

All of a sudden, Moonshiners didn't seem quite so dorky.

Rope Drop

As they stepped off the monorail, Eric was greeted by a number of subtle changes. The station seemed older; not physically, but more in a thematic sense. The music was different, too. It was laid back, but he couldn't quite place what it represented.

As they walked down the path, another Monorail rolled over their heads on the elevated track. In the distance, he could see a large boat pulling into its dock. Off to the side, there were smaller boats arriving and departing.

He passed through the gate first. He waived his wrist over a globe, which lit up and he was allowed to pass. Next, he waited as a member of security looked in Sally's purse. He narrowed his eyes at that exchange. It had to be the worst search he had ever seen. The cast member did next to nothing. He could have smuggled a gun in with no effort.

"Do you have a camera on you?" asked an average looking tourist.

He looked at him and said he did not.

"Do you have two cell phones then?"

This question put him on alert. Why would this guy ask that?

"No. I only have one," Eric said as he stared down the man.

"Then what's in your other pocket," the man asked as he pulled out his ID, which showed he was a cast member in the security department.

He smiled and pulled out his badge.

"Well done!" Eric said as he caught on to what was happening.

"The bag search is just a ruse, isn't it?"

"Not really. It is an active deterrent, but as you figured, the real security is where you are not looking. We look for body language and things that don't look right. It's ten times more effective than searching a bag. Almost anyone who wants to do something wrong knows how to avoid the bag search."

He wondered why the airports didn't do that. Few things were more asinine than going through airport security. As a member of law enforcement, it took him a whole two seconds to find a number of flaws that could be exploited. Most of all, the whole random search policy TSA had was a massive waste of time. Monitoring and responding to behavior was far more effective than a metal detector. He now understood why there had never been an attack at the number one vacation destination in the world. Unlike the TSA, Disney didn't suffer from cranial-rectal inversion.

He followed Sally and Matt as they walked over to one of the tunnels and waited. He started to ask himself why anyone would get here so early only to wait. He looked over at his friends. He could tell from the looks on their faces that they knew the answer.

"Why are we here so early?"

Sally looked at him and said, "It's rope drop, suga."

After seeing the confused look on his face she explained, "The cast members are holding a rope across the pathway to hold everyone back. When the park opens they will walk up Main Street USA. At the entrances to the other lands are other sets of cast members who have another rope to intercept any people headed into that land. They will walk them to the E-Tickets at a safe pace. Oh, E-Tickets are the most popular rides."

"Why would you need to do that? Just drop the rope and let them go."

Matt let out one of his rumbling laughs and said, "They used to do that. I think they had to start giving hazard pay to cast members holding the rope. None of them were ever seriously injured, but I heard that every now and then one of them ended up in the hospital after getting trampled.

"You also have to remember that some people can't be trusted with their own safety. Disney doesn't like having to put guests back together on the first day of their vacations after they fall and land on their faces. Banged up people spend less.

"Thankfully, it's January. It's one of the slowest times of the year. You should see this place in the summer."

As Eric looked around at the growing crowd he started to get nervous. If this was a small crowd he had no desire to see a large one.

What had he gotten himself into?

"What's our game plan?" Sally asked as she rubbed her hands together.

He turned to her and explained, "I've got a touring plan and schedule. We are going to Space Mountain first. I should have grabbed a map, though. I'm not sure where it is."

Sally cocked her head and said, "We don't need no map, suga. You's with the pros!"

An announcement was made welcoming everyone to the Magic Kingdom. With one accord, the crowd surged forward and through the tunnel. On the walls were colorful posters for the various rides. He thought that was odd. Why would you advertise after people had already paid?

They surged through the tunnel and what his senses relayed to his brain nearly overwhelmed him. He caught a strong scent of popcorn. He heard music that seemed like it fit in the 18th century. When he looked around, he could have sworn he'd been teleported to another world. Everything he saw told him he was in the 1900s. From the gas lamps to the architecture, from the horse-pulled trolley to the barbershop quartet, he had traveled back in time.

The crowd surged around a small garden area and started down Main Street USA.

This time what he saw stopped him in his tracks. The amazing re-creation of 1900s America faded away to a castle with high turrets. The multi-pronged assault on his senses was overwhelming. He'd never experienced anything like this. He could feel tears welling up in his eyes.

Sally reached out and grabbed his hand to pull him along. He smiled as he realized she may have just saved his life from the charging crowd.

Suddenly, a melancholy feeling washed over him. In his mind's eye he could see the exact thing happening 48 hours earlier, when Javon and his family had come through this very walkway.

Space Mountain

"Come on, suga! We need to get as close to the front as we can!" Sally cried as she kicked her chunky legs into overdrive.

"Why the rush?" Eric asked as he was dragged along.

Matt, who was already breaking a sweat from the physical exertion chimed in, "Space Mountain has been one of the most popular rides in the Magic Kingdom since it opened. If we get there within a few minutes we can almost walk on. In an hour or so the wait will be up to 30 to 60 minutes."

He couldn't imagine anyone waiting that long for a ride, but wisely didn't argue the point.

They veered to the right as they drew closer to the castle. They charged over a bridge and then under a sign that said "Tomorrowland." It was round with funny looking laser-like appendages coming out of it. It looked like they designed it to give the impression it came out of a cartoon or 1950s sci-fi movie.

They officially entered Tomorrowland. On both sides were buildings with blue and silver façades.

If Sally had not had a vice grip on his hand, he would have stopped when he saw a trashcan moving. He could have sworn he heard it talking, too.

"Was that trash can talking?!?"

"Yeah, suga. You can see it later. It's meant to thin and distract the crowd," Sally yelled back as she continued to push forward.

The crowd thinned more as they passed Stitch's Great Escape, Monsters, Inc. Laugh Floor, and Astro Orbiter.

When they passed a Buzz Lightyear ride he figured out where they were going. Before them was an intimidating, white, pyramid-shaped building, with what almost looked like lightning rods at the pinnacle.

As they got closer, he could see two times displayed. One listed the Fastpass return time. The other showed the standby time as being five minutes.

"Awesome! No wait!" Matt cried as they surged into the queue.

Finally they slowed down, now that they were in the queue. He took the opportunity to state, "The sign said five minutes."

"That's just Disney for no wait. When you see a wait time, cut it in half." Sally said with authority.

"Why would they post a time that is double the actual wait?"

"If you are willing to wait twenty minutes and only end up

waiting ten, you feel like you got lucky. At the same time, if you wait twenty, you are not disappointed. If you wait longer, you will be upset. By posting a longer time, Disney is hedging their bets. This way, they will exceed or at least meet your expectations."

As they progressed down the queue, daylight faded away and was replaced by a soft blue light that seemed to come up from underneath the walkway they were on. To the left and right there were windows that seemed to look out into space. As they continued down the queue, they passed what looked like a video game on the left. After the video game screens, the queue started to rise. When it split, the three of them went to the right.

He could see that there were multiple boarding stations, one on either side of the tunnel they had just exited. He could also hear screams echoing off the walls and ceiling above him. The ceiling had projections of asteroids floating across it.

They followed the line, which by passed long, deep switchbacks.

"Wow, I would not want to wait in those," he said to himself.

Matt laughed and explained, "If that's all you have to wait through you're lucky. On busy days, the wait can hit 120 minutes and the line spills outside."

That statement dumbfounded him. What kind of ride was

worth waiting for two hours? That was insane. It almost seemed like this line could corral more people than some theme parks held in their entirety.

They reached the end of the line. A cast member asked how many were in their group and then directed them to numbers on the floor.

There were two people on similar numbers in front of him. As the small trains, designed to look like small spaceships, arrived, the first group would get on, everyone stepped forward to the next set of numbers, and his anticipation grew.

When it was time for him to step off the platform he was almost intimidated.

Why? He'd ridden monster roller coasters before. This would be nothing, so why was he anxious? Then it hit him; he didn't see the track. All he heard were screams.

He sat down on the uncomfortable seat and put the safety gear in place. He was in the front seat with Matt behind him and Sally in the third.

From behind, Matt leaned forward, put his hands on his shoulders and jokingly shook him as he yelled out.

Everyone was laughing when the cast member pushed a button and the vehicle lurched forward.

They whipped through a small tunnel and hit the lift hill. On the right was a parallel track, with another vehicle ascending it. Between the two tracks was a very detailed scene of an astronaut on a spacewalk. Above them, asteroids flew through the sky.

They reached the top of the hill and their vehicle was released. It went around a corner and entered almost complete darkness. All they could see were the glowing sides of the other trains and the asteroids overhead.

Sally sounded like she was screaming and laughing at the same time. Every time they hit a turn or dip, her volume increased.

They sped through the darkness, at what felt like a colossal rate of speed. Suddenly, they plummeted down and everyone let out a scream. They entered a tunnel. There was a flash and then a thunderous boom.

They turned a corner and the vehicle jerked as it hit the breaks. They'd reached the end.

A few minutes later, they stood in front of some video monitors. Matt had known there was an on-ride photo. The big jerk had leaned forward, made a silly face and given Eric bunny ears. He looked like a boob with a funny expression on his face.

Sally, who also knew about the photo, was looking right at the camera. She had a hand over her mouth as if she was surprised. Her other hand was pointing at them.

The jerks had planned it.

Of course, they bought the photo.

Bears and Mermaids

They left Space Mountain and made a beeline for the Many Adventures of Winnie the Pooh. To get there, they walked out the backside of Tomorrowland. On the way, they passed the Tomorrowland Speedway. Eric looked at his plan and was glad he didn't have to ride that thing. It stood out like a sore thumb. It was loud and smelly. Considering everything else he'd seen, he couldn't imagine why the attraction existed here. He also couldn't figure out what made it futuristic. In the end, he just figured there was nowhere else to put it so they stuck it here. It seemed like a total waste of space.

As they transitioned from Tmorrowland to Fantasyland, the music shifted from the funky sounds of a proposed future to something that seemed like the soundtrack of Sleeping Beauty or Cinderella.

They entered the queue for the Pooh ride. To say it was interesting was an understatement. It had been designed with an interactive area for kids. That was a novel idea. Keep the kids distracted while the parents waited in line. He figured that was a blessing for the parents. The batteries in an iPod only lasted so long. With a queue like this, the parents could stretch them longer.

He thought back to going to theme parks when he was a kid. He remembered waiting in lines with nothing but his imagination for entertainment. Those lines were boring switchbacks, too. No theming or distraction. God, kids today were lucky.

He smirked when he saw the ride vehicles. They looked like big honey pots. It was a nice touch. They could have just put a bland glorified box with seats in, but they didn't. They went the extra mile.

As they went through the ride it only took a couple of minutes for a powerful sense of nostalgia to hit him. He knew this story. They had recreated and converted "The Blustery Day" into a 3D attraction. As they continued, a growing sense of awe settled upon him as he noticed one tiny detail from the story after another.

He was startled when their ride vehicle started bouncing to coincide with the Tigger scene. He never would have expected something like that.

"Where are we going next?" asked Sally, as they got off the ride.

He looked at his touring plan and said, "Under the Sea."

Sally gasped and charged off, "You're gonna love it!" she cried over her shoulder.

As they walked, Eric opened up the "Lines" app on his iPhone. He navigated to *Under the Sea* to see if by chance anyone had reported an up-to-date wait time. He was shocked. Two different people had already reported. The most recent was only ten minutes by someone with a username of "funmunke."

He shook his head. People came up with the craziest usernames. What kind of a tool named himself funmunke? At least it wasn't offensive or racist. It was amazing how many times during an investigation that he or Jose would stumble across a horrible screen name or username. More often than not it seemed like someone's username was a true representation of that person. Like Jose, for instance, he often used the screen name MxicnThndr. It always made him laugh, but it was such a fitting moniker when you saw Jose in action.

They came to *Under the Sea* and he slowed down a little. What he saw before him looked like it had exploded off the movie screen and into real life. He had seen this before, but in a cartoon. All the details were the same. This was from *The Little Mermaid.*

His anticipation was high as he sat down in the ride vehicle. His grandmother had taken him to see *The Little Mermaid* in the theater when he was a little kid. He was so young, it was one of the first memories he could recall. Every time he thought of that movie he thought of his now deceased grandmother.

It was brutally hard for him to keep his emotions in check as the ride progressed. All of the famous scenes and musical numbers were represented in the ride, in stunning detail. Even Ursula was there. She was massive, and had many moving parts that functioned so smoothly, it almost seemed that she was alive.

By the time the ride was over, he was a little dazed.

Boys and Ghosts

Their next stop was on the far side of Fantasyland. It was some Peter Pan ride. Eric pulled up Lines to see it already had a 15-minute wait.

"This is one of the best dark rides in all of Disney World!" Matt stated emphatically. "Ever since they ruined Imagination, this one is solidly in the top three!"

He glanced at Sally to see if Matt was exaggerating, but she was wholeheartedly nodding her head in agreement.

He was really enjoying himself so far, so he decided to goad Matt a little.

"What's so great about it?"

Matt tried his best to explain why it stood out. After a few minutes the only thing that sounded interesting to him was the track. Apparently you hung suspended from the track instead of riding on top of it. That worried him a little. It seemed like a lot weight hanging on something he couldn't see, but he figured it was safe considering how long it had been in operation.

By the time they got to the ride, the line was wrapped around a series of switchbacks. Looking at the queue, he figured this area hadn't changed much since the ride opened. It didn't fit in with the other queues he had seen.

When they reached the front of the line he wondered why it had taken so long. This thing was a people eater. It never stopped. To board, you stepped onto a moving walkway and then into the vehicle. There must have been far more people in front of them than he had taken note of.

After they had stepped off the ride, he had to agree with his friends. It was a fun little ride. He now understood what they had meant by a "dark ride." The whole thing had been lit up by black lights. The glowing paint had given the ride a surreal look, which was only enhanced by the fact that you seemed to be flying over everything in a pirate ship.

They crossed from Fantasyland into a land called Liberty Square. Again, everything shifted. The general atmosphere reminded him of parts of Boston. The buildings took on the look of those built in the mid- to late 1700s. As they walked under a tree with a number of lanterns hanging on it, Eric noticed that the music had changed to more of a colonial feel. It reminded him of Yankee Doodle Dandy.

He took a moment to imagine what Javon must have been experiencing. After what he had been through, how would he have felt?

He looked around at some of the children in the area and figured it out. He saw a number of kids who almost looked like they were in a daze, but somehow there were no upset ones. If he didn't know any better, he would have said the kids around him were high.

It took a moment, but he grasped what they were feeling. They most likely had never been so over stimulated by their surroundings. All of the feelings it generated were positive, though. That kind of stimulation would naturally release serotonin, noradrenaline, and dopamine into your bloodstream and brain. Considering that, they really were high, albeit naturally.

He heard their next stop before he saw it, as a wolf howled. He looked over to see his friends grinning. For a moment he thought he should remind them that they were supposed to be the parents, but when he looked around he saw a vast majority of the parents in the area looked like his friends.

They entered the queue for the Haunted Mansion. As they did, they passed an old horse-drawn hearse, except in place of a horse, a saddle and tack were floating in the air. He smiled at the illusion; a ghost horse. It was so simple, yet effective.

They passed a number of gravestones with rhyming sayings engraved on them like, "Here lays Fred. A big rock dropped on his head."

The final gravestone was just creepy. It had a woman's face engraved on it. As he looked at it the eyes opened and looked right at him.

They waited for a moment, and then the doors before them swung open. A stern looking cast member stood there and invited everyone in. They passed through a dimly lit room with a painting of a normal looking man that dissolved into a corpse as Eric watched.

The next room was round with no doors. On the walls above some wooden paneling and ornate gargoyles were several paintings of people who looked like they were from the early 1900s.

He jumped when the cast member behind him yelled out, "Please move to the DEAD center of the room!"

The wall swung shut behind the cast member and a voice came on. The room started to stretch. The paintings shifted up to show that what had been displayed were just fragments of scenes of people in great peril .

Suddenly, the room went black and a bolt of lightning flashed. The lights came on and one of the walls on the far side of the room slid aside.

It took a minute for the crowd to pour through the opening. He took the opportunity to stand in the middle of the room and take it all in. The detail was over the top.

Suddenly, he heard something that made the hair on the back of his neck stand up. It was whispering. He looked at the cast member who only smiled. The whispering seemed to be coming from all over.

"You just stumbled across one of Disney World's best kept

secrets, suga!" Sally called out from the door.

"Most people are so intent on moving forward, they are never in this room long enough to hear the gargoyles whisper to each other."

The rest of the ride amazed him. It relied heavily on very old optical illusions and tricks. It occurred to Eric that despite all the advances in technology, these simple illusions were far more effective since they were real, instead of digital recreations.

The end of the ride left him laughing. Across from him was a mirrored wall. He watched as a "ghost" appeared on the wall, pulled his beard off and stuck it on Sally. With her short chunky frame, the beard made her look like a dwarf from the Lord of the Rings.

Wet Lunch

"When do we eat? I'm starving!" Matt bellyached as they entered Frontierland.

Eric was astonished that anyone could be hungry after that breakfast. He pulled out his iPhone and checked his plan.

"We need to grab a Fastpass for Big Thunder Mountain and then ride Splash Mountain," he responded.

"Ooooo! Splash is the best ride in Disney World!" Sally exclaimed.

Matt disagreed with Sally's assessment and suddenly, he found himself in the middle of a war of words. They went back and forth arguing the drawbacks and benefits of a number of rides, and why one was better than another. They kept bickering as they passed a launch to *Tom Sawyer's Island*, a log building that housed the *Country Bear Jamboree*, and a cart selling monstrous turkey legs that looked like they were straight out of the *Flintstones*.

By the time they reached the Fastpass machines for Big Thunder Mountain, they had stopped talking to each other and an uncomfortable silence ensued. It occurred to him that this was actually very helpful. He remembered from his family vacations as a kid that at some point his parents would get into a disagreement. He remembered sitting in the back seat of their car with his sister, while his parents went at it in the front. It was never anything serious, but the stress involved with getting kids from point "A" to point "B" always took a toll.

He could easily imagine Javon's parents arguing about something as they made their way through the park. He made a mental note to keep a lookout for other parents doing just that.

It didn't take long. As they neared the entrance to the queue for Splash Mountain he spotted a … lively discussion. Someone who appeared to be the mother was growling at her husband. He heard the mother say, "I wanted to sit in the back for a reason!" as they passed by. That's when he noticed that the woman was drenched from head to toe and her makeup was streaking. In fact, the entire family was soaked as well. The husband and kids didn't seem to mind, but the mother was livid.

He wondered if she fell off the ride into a pool or something, when he passed a warning sign that stated: "You will get wet."

As they climbed the final lift hill, he had to agree with Sally. This had to be one of the best rides in Disney World. He hadn't seen all of the rides yet, but between the story, characters, music, lighting, and layout this had to be the best ride he had ever seen.

As they crested the top of the hill a sudden question popped into his head. Why had Sally and Matt insisted that he sit in front of them? His experience on Space Mountain popped into his head and he figured it out. There must be a ride photo coming!

He was not going to be caught off guard this time. As they started to drop he made the ugliest face he could and stuck a finger up his nose.

When they hit the bottom of the chute he realized his assumption had been wrong.

A massive spray of water shot up and hit him in the face. It soaked him to the bone.

Those jerks did it again. They used him as a human shield and ended up with a very incriminating photo of him in the process.

ME MAN! EAT MEAT!...and Pineapple

Eric pulled up the notes on his phone to see what Javon and his family had done for lunch. They had stopped at two places. The first was the cart that he had seen earlier. They had bought turkey legs.

When the cast member handed him the smoked turkey leg he couldn't help but smile. He could swear that there were barbells at his gym that weighed less than this thing. The leg was so large he could easily use it as a club to defend himself if he had to.

Matt held out his leg and growled, "ME MAN! EAT MEAT" before he tore off a huge chunk of meat with a roar.

"Don't be a pig!" Sally scolded him, but that only seemed to encourage the man.

Eric hesitantly took a bite. He was amazed. He had expected the leg to be tough and utterly unpleasant. Instead, it was rather tender and had great flavor.

"This is one of the best deals in Disney," Matt sputtered out through a mouthful of food.

Sally gave him a dirty look and put a hand on her hip, "Don't talk with your mouth full!"

Matt just gave her a big stupid grin as he continued to

assault his turkey leg.

There were no available places to sit nearby so they ate standing up. As he stood there, he took note of how many people went through that cart. These carts had to go through a staggering number of turkey legs throughout the day. They only offered legs, so he assumed one, or possibly many, of the restaurants served some of the other turkey parts.

For the second course, they headed into Adventureland. Once again, there was a subtle shift in everything as they transitioned from one land to another. Most theme parks played the same music across the entire park. Disney was very different. Each land seemed to have its own distinct soundtrack.

When they arrived at their destination, Sally said, "They certainly searched out the best things! Nothing cools you off like a Dole Whip."

"I don't care what they ordered, suga. You need to get yourself a pineapple Dole Whip float. It's basically pineapple ice cream in pineapple juice. It's the best!"

Eric sat down nearby and took a bite. He wasn't a big pineapple fan, but this was really good. He realized that it was a nice offset to the salty turkey leg. He thought about Javon eating this and realized that the kid must have gotten a major sugar rush if he ate the entire thing. Considering how tired he was already, he didn't doubt he was going to need that sugar rush to push forward.

He was suddenly aware that a lot of people around him were smoking. He realized he was in a smoking area. Why would Disney turn one of the few places to sit down in the area into a smoking spot? The fact it was right next to a food counter made it an even stranger choice. In the end he figured it had to go somewhere. At least it was off to the side.

There and Back Again

The afternoon was filled with zigzagging across the park and back again. The assortment of rides was staggering. Eric made notes as they went. He figured he'd show them to Matt and Sally after to give them a good laugh. He was sure anyone who'd been to Disney would understand them:

- Pirates of the Caribbean – I never knew pirates liked redheads so much

- Big Thunder Mountain – Wimpy roller coaster with awesome theming

- Hall of Presidents – Thank god, I needed a nap.

- Jungle Cruise – That "skipper" needed to lay off the coffee

- Country Bear Jamboree – "Blood on the sand ..."

- Enchanted Tiki Room – Sing like the birds. Click, Click, Click

- Swiss Family Treehouse – Don't tell the ADA!

- Mickey's PhilharMagic – My head hurts now and I can't uncross my eyes.

- Mad Tea Party – Should be sponsored by Dramamine.

- Walt Disney World Railroad – The train wasn't the only thing that tooted.

- Monsters, Inc. Laugh Floor – Do I really have to buy everyone chalupas?

- Buzz Lightyear – That gun was broken! I'm a much better shot than that!

For dinner they headed back to the end of Main Street, USA. There stood the Crystal Palace. He had to pull strings to get into this place. Apparently it was so popular that some people made reservations for it up to 120 days in advance. Who did that? Even if you were on vacation, who really knew where they were going to be that far in advance? You'd almost have to plan your day based on where you wanted to eat.

He could hear Buddy's voice echo in his head again, "*It's Disney.*" He guessed the normal rules didn't really apply to anything here.

He approached the check-in podium. The cast member asked him if he had an ADR. He didn't know why Disney didn't just call them reservations, like everyone else on Earth. "Reservation" wasn't any harder to say than ADR. It was even more foolish when you found out that ADR stood for "Advance Dining Reservation." It was just Disney trying to be different.

Maybe that was the point all along. People were used to

"reservations." If you didn't think about it, ADR sounded special or important. The more he thought about it, the more he realized how genius that was.

Once they were seated, he looked around. This place was a madhouse. It was bursting at the seams and it was loud. The noise level wasn't helped by the fact that there were a handful of characters walking around and visiting the tables.

He wished he had looked up this place in advance so he could have prepared himself for the food. It was a buffet. He hated buffets.

At a wedding or catered event they were fine. When he was paying, they were not. If he was going to pay for a meal in a restaurant he wanted to relax. He didn't want to have to navigate a crowd and then slap some mediocre food onto his plate from a bin that had most likely been sneezed on half a dozen times and prepared by someone who didn't know how to wash his hands after dropping a deuce.

At least buffets were cheap. Which was at least some compensation for the terrible bout of dysentery that usually followed eating at one.

Well, they were supposed to be cheap. He never knew that if you threw a few people into giant animal suits you could charge twice the price and still pack the place.

After he managed to navigate to the buffet and back he felt a little better. The food, while not amazing, seemed to be better than average. The majority of it seemed like it was really cooked, not just reheated.

An excited cry caused him to look up from his plate. Matt was pointing his camera at he and Sally. He thought it was an odd time for a photo but he smiled anyway. That's when he felt a padded hand on his shoulder. He snapped his head around to see Tigger hamming it up behind him. Now he understood why there had been a cry of excitement.

He knew there was just a person in that costume, but he couldn't help but feel excited. He found himself giggling as Tigger went through his antics. The whole scene was repeated again and again as Pooh, Piglet and Eeyore came and went.

Suddenly, there was an announcement and the cast members gathered kids and put them with the characters. Some music started and they all started to march around the dining room.

A young African American boy caught his eye. Even though he knew it was not Javon, his mind caused him to hallucinate.

Time seemed to slow down and he watched as Javon laughed and skipped about. He saw him look back and wave to his parents as Pooh led him by the hand. He could see his mom stand up and take a photo while his father waved back, as he recorded the whole thing on a camcorder.

"Oh my, are you ok, suga?"

Sally's question broke his trance. When he snapped out of it, he realized tears had streaked down his cheeks. All he could do was sit there and nod.

M.I.C.K.E.Y. M.O.U.S.E.

Throughout the day, a lot of things that Eric had thought were odd explained themselves. He seriously doubted this one would.

They had used Fastpass for rides like *Big Thunder Mountain* and the *Jungle Cruise*, but this made no sense.

"I still don't understand why we need a Fastpass to meet Mickey Mouse."

"Dude! Mickey is the reason! This place *exists* because of him. He was Walt's greatest accomplishment. He's the ultimate E-Ticket!" Matt explained.

He guessed it made sense but he had to ask, "What's an E-Ticket again?"

Sally nodded and explained, "It's something that no longer exists, but became a definition we still use. It's like how we call musical releases "albums.

"Disney abandoned E-Tickets years before any of us ever stepped foot in the parks. When Disney World first opened, you didn't buy admission, you bought a book of tickets. They were broken down in tickets labeled A through E. You got a lot of "A" tickets. They were trivial things. The better rides got better tickets. The best of the best got an "E" ticket. You only got a few of those in the book."

The line that Fastpass allowed them to bypass was astonishing. He couldn't believe how long people were willing to wait to meet the Mouse.

Suddenly, he almost felt guilty. He felt like he was cutting the line. Of course in reality he was, but Fastpass allowed it. Still, he felt bad as he saw all the kids waiting in that huge line.

He also noticed something important to his research. It was getting late in the day. A lot of the kids looked wrecked. Some were barely standing, others were passed out cold in strollers or their parent's arms.

He really cringed as he noticed a few kids suffer total meltdowns. Those families looked like they'd been through a war. Suddenly he remembered the nap he took in the *Hall of Presidents*. He might be melting down now too, if not for that nap. He suddenly cursed his touring plan. It was a plan for families with tweens. There should have been a nap built in. Any family that didn't get a break in that schedule was going to crash at some point.

It looked like a lot of families were at that point.

It then occurred to him that he had made a mistake. He should never have let himself take a nap. He had seen nothing that implied Javon had taken a nap. It was also very unlikely a ten year old was going to take a nap by his own accord while at the Magic Kingdom.

Despite his best efforts, he couldn't help but smile as he approached Mickey. When he got close he heard something that stopped him in his tracks.

"Are you having a magical day, Eric?"

He was shocked. The question came from Mickey. It wasn't someone inside Mickey either. It was Mickey's voice that asked it. All he could do was stammer out a yes.

"The Polynesian is great, isn't it?" came Mickey's voice again.

He was really getting unsettled. How could this be possible?

He looked down and figured it out when he saw his wrist. The RFID in his wristband must have triggered the interactions.

He laughed and realized that a kid wouldn't have figured that out. To a kid this would have been pure magic.

Wishes

As he walked out of the meet and greet building, Eric realized they were almost done with their day. He now had a slight challenge. He had to find where Javon and his family had stopped to watch the fireworks. All he had was a photo taken during show to help him find the location. He grabbed his phone and pulled up the photo.

"Do either of you know where this would have been taken from?" he asked as he turned toward his friends.

Matt and Sally looked at the photo and to his delight, they nodded.

"I sure do. It's an alternative spot to watch the fireworks. Most people pack onto Main Street, or pile on top of each other in front of the castle. If you want a more laid back experience, without people crowding you, you go here. It's a spot in between the area in front of the castle and Tomorrowland. Just follow me," Matt said as he charged off.

In few minutes, he was sure he was standing within inches of where Javon and his family had been standing just 48 hours earlier. It offered a nice view of the castle. Something else caught his attention. It smelled nice. Many areas of the park had a certain smell that went with them, but this one stood out. He looked around and noticed that there were a lot rose bushes planted in the area. The smell had a calming effect.

An announcement came over the loudspeakers and a light show started on the castle. This light show was almost mind bending. Somehow, they made the contoured surface appear almost flat as they bounced all sorts of photos and animations off of it. He figured they must have digitally mapped the castle and then warped the photos being displayed to create the illusion.

"It's wild isn't it, suga?" Sally asked.

"It's called the *Magic, Memories, and You*. Sometimes if you are very lucky they put a picture of you up there with all the others."

The show only lasted a few minutes. When it ended, the castle went dark and everyone cheered.

What happened next made his jaw drop.

At the very top of the castle a figure lit up. At first he thought it was just a mannequin of Tinker Bell but then it started to move as it pushed away from the castle.

Tinker Bell flew directly over his head and only then did he notice the zip line above him. She flew off in the direction of Tomorrowland and disappeared out of sight.

The fireworks started. The entire show was set to the music he had heard the previous night on the beach at the

Polynesian. Today, however, he could more accurately see that the colors, and even the shape of the explosions were set to a story.

The show pressed on. Its feel went from happy to scary and back again. In the end, the good guys won out and this was celebrated when a huge finale was set off. The entire night sky lit up with exploding fireworks, and then it was over.

Ears

Eric knew they were not quite ready to leave. They had one more stop before the day was complete.

They slowly made their way down Main Street, USA. The crowd working its way toward the exit was almost wall to wall. There were no extended hours tonight, so everyone was leaving at the same time.

They fought their way to the right. It took a few minutes, but they finally reached the sidewalk. Right before them was their destination.

"*The Emporium*" was a huge gift shop with multiple entrances. He knew from his notes that Javon's parents had told him in advance that they were not going to buy any souvenirs. What Javon didn't know was that his parents were just kidding. All along they had decided they were going to buy him a special gift. They had planned it out because their gift required some custom work.

He could only imagine the look on Javon's face when his parents brought him into the Emporium and a cast member handed him a pair of mouse ears with his name embroidered on them.

He stopped at the entrance, when he was bombarded by mixed emotions. Although he knew this wasn't going to be easy, he pushed through the door and stepped in.

The sheer number of souvenirs in the shop was staggering. It seemed like Disney had thought of every possible souvenir, and then some. There were dozens of different hats, including Matt's nerdy monorail hat. There were t-shirts, sweatshirts, hoodies, jackets, and more. There was even a set of Mickey Mouse slippers that were identical to the yellow shoes Mickey wore.

He looked at some of the displays and wondered who would buy some of this stuff. Who would want Disney housewares?

Sally cried out, "Oooooo! A Mickey Mouse shaker!"

He had his answer. Sally didn't even drink, but she was willing to buy a cocktail shaker because it had mouse ears on it.

He reached the counter and told the cast member his name. The cast member left and then returned with a pair of mouse ears.

He had a hard time building up the willpower to reach out and take them. As he held them is his hand, the image of a pair of mouse ears lying at the edge of a pool of blood appeared in his head. Unwittingly, he turned the mouse ears over in his hands, looking for the stain he knew wasn't there.

Slowly he put the ears on his head.

Matt smiled at him and said, "They look good on you. Maybe I should trade in my hat for a pair."

"I don't think they come in your size," Sally laughed.

"Sometimes you forget you're almost as big as Sweetums. You look like him too!" he joked, referring to the monstrous shaggy Muppet.

"Hey, you made a Disney reference!" Matt exclaimed.

"What? Sweetums isn't Disney, he's one of the Muppets."

"Yeah, but Disney owns the Muppets!"

Eric gave up; he didn't have the energy or desire to discuss something so ridiculous.

As they exited the shop, Sally slid one arm through Matt's and the other through his own.

"Well, look at me. I'm sandwiched between my Sweetums and Mickey Mouse. No one's gonna be messin with me tonight!"

The Final Moments of Javon Jones

The line for the monorail was quite long. Eric was just happy they were getting on the resort monorail. The line for the express monorail was twice as long.

Despite the line, it didn't take too long for them to get on. This time they were packed in, but it still wasn't anywhere near as bad as a packed "T" in Boston.

"I like your ears."

He looked down to see a young boy seated on the bench. He was wearing a Mickey Mouse t-shirt and a pair of mouse ears.

At first he couldn't respond. It took a minute for his brain to kick in and tell him he was not looking at Javon's ghost.

"Thanks, but I think yours are better," he told the boy who smiled back at him.

"Are you staying on site?" asked a woman next to the boy, who he took for the mother.

"Yes. I'm staying at the Polynesian."

"We were there, but they moved us to the Contemporary. I still can't believe what happened. We were in the room across the hall," the mother said, her voice cracking.

"Did you hear anything?"

The mother just shook her head before saying, "Just the mother screaming when they found him.

"I opened the door to see what was going on," a man standing in front of the mother explained, "I was the one who called 911."

Eric pulled out his business card and handed it to them. "I've been assigned to the case. If you think of anything let me know. Even if you think it's nothing or a trivial detail. Sometimes the smallest things turn out to be very important."

The family thanked him and stood up. He had been so distracted he hadn't even realized that they had pulled into the Contemporary.

He was silent, lost in his own thoughts, as they arrived and departed from the Ticket and Transportation Center. Neither Sally nor Matt said anything. They just let him think.

Matt and Sally leaned on each other as they staggered down the path to the Tokelau building. He knew how they felt. He had run half marathons and felt better than this after. His legs felt like rubber and his feet felt like they had swollen up a whole shoe size. He pulled out his iPhone and pulled up his "FitBit" app. The phone communicated with the bracelet on his left arm. He hoped the Disney

RFID bracelet on his right arm wouldn't interfere with the signal.

After a few seconds the data populated onto his phone. He eyes widened as he looked at the totals before him. He had walked 10.2 miles and taken 21,034 steps. No wonder his feet hurt.

They made it back to the abandoned building and stepped into their room. He wondered how Javon had any energy left after that day, as he sat down on the edge of the bed and turned on the TV.

The slightly nasally voice of Stacey Aswad blared from the TV. At first, he wondered how anyone could watch this obnoxious show. Within minutes, that thought had completely disappeared from his head. Her energy was infectious. She hit up one Disney headliner after another. Before he knew it, he was captivated.

Suddenly, his alarm went off. He looked over and nodded to Matt and Sally. They picked up their mugs and left the room.

When they made it back to the room, they found him sitting on the floor in front of the door with his mouse ears lying sideways next to him. He was weeping uncontrollably.

It took several minutes for him to compose himself enough to choke out, "He died on the best day of his life."

Frustration

Jose pulled his chest up to the bar. In one explosive motion, he shot his hands up and forced the bar up and onto the next two pegs on the obstacle called the "Salmon Ladder." With a grunt, he repeated the process again and again until he reached the top. The group watching from the side of the pool broke out into a cheer. Only three of them could make it to the top of the salmon ladder, and none of them as fast as Jose.

He hung there a second before releasing his grip and falling into the pool below. He'd been training on the various obstacles for over an hour now. Mostly, he was trying to clear his head. Often the only place he could go to just forget everything was this gym, with its intense obstacles.

No matter what he did, nothing seemed to help tonight. He'd spent the entire day researching the murder victim's parents, to no avail. After many hours, he'd come away with nothing that seemed like it would be useful. He had only been able to find run-of-the-mill info. For all intents and purposes, the Jones family was just ... normal. There was no history of mental illness, no large insurance policies, no financial or marital problems; there was nothing to explain why they would kill their child.

Some of the guys slapped him on the back as he walked by. He knew what he was going to try next.

"You gonna try the cliffhanger!?!" one of the guys asked.

He just nodded as he headed over to one of the most difficult obstacles the sadistic designers at Ninja Warrior had ever thought up.

Anyone who looked at the cliffhanger had the same first impression. It should be impossible. He would agree with them, if he hadn't seen it conquered on TV.

The entire gym gathered to watch.

He put his fingers on the one-inch lip and swung his body away from the platform. Slowly, he inched his way across the first lip. A lot of people didn't even make it this far. Holding your entire body weight by your finger was one thing, working your way across five feet like that was torturous. Doing the same thing on a one-inch lip that slanted up ...

He reached the end of the first five feet and everyone cheered. Slowly, he reached up a few inches and grasped the second slanted expanse. The guys on the floor cheered him on as he slowly made his way up. He finally reached the top.

The next transition was a larger reach, but at least the next lip wasn't slanted, it was just long.

Now ten feet off the ground, he inched his way across the ten foot lip. By the time he made it to the end, his forearms were screaming.

The next transition was the worst one yet. He had to hold on with one hand as he reached across and up a one-foot gap. With a grunt he pushed himself and managed to lock onto the next lip.

The entire gym was cheering him on now. They wanted to see one of their own conquer this, so they'd know that with practice they might be able to do the same someday.

The next section was why many considered the cliffhanger to be impossible.

The next step was a three-foot gap. It was impossible to reach across while maintaining your grip. You had to throw yourself across the gap and then catch yourself — on a one- inch lip that was barely the length of a man's hand-width.

Slowly, Jose started to swing his legs back and forth to gain momentum. After a couple of seconds, he exploded across the gap. He made it to the lip. He'd never managed to get the distance right in the past. All he had to do now was stop his momentum and hold himself up.

His fingers slipped off the lip and he crashed to the cushions below.

As he lay there, it occurred to him that his failure aptly mirrored the day he'd just had. It had started with hope and ended in disappointment.

He slammed his fists into the cushions and decided he'd had enough for one day.

Utilidors

"I need to talk to a security expert, someone who knows a lot about the RFID readers, and Mickey Mouse," Eric told his contact at Disney. He felt almost hung-over after recreating Javon's last day. It didn't help that he had barely slept last night. His brain had refused to turn off. Overloaded with information and stimuli, his brain had kicked into overdrive in an effort to process it all.

He was told to check in at the front gate of the Magic Kingdom. Someone would meet him there.

He arrived at the prearranged spot an hour later, and was greeted by an older guy with salt and pepper hair.

"Are you Detective Highland?"

He nodded and provided his badge and ID. The guy shook his hand and introduced himself as Victor Webb.

"We are headed down to our command center in the Utilidors."

He was too tired to even bother to ask what a "utilidor" was. He followed Victor into the Magic Kingdom and up to a nondescript door, that looked like it was a fake entrance to one of the buildings. It was the last of three such doors. The genius of putting an actual door here made him smile.

Not only did all three look fake, but if anyone tried the first one they would never have continued down the line to try all three.

What was behind the door was very un-Disney. The room was as utilitarian as you could get. Everything was nondescript and bland. Even the lighting was boring. Basic fluorescent lights lined the ceiling.

He followed Victor around a corner to a set of stairs.

"Ha! I never figured this place had a basement," he said.

"Well it doesn't really," Victor said smiling.

"What do you mean?"

"Did you ever notice that you walk up an incline as you approach the front gate?"

He hadn't thought about it before, but there was a subtle incline. He nodded at Victor to continue.

"Well, when they built this place they actually started with the corridors we are about to descend into. Then they built the Magic Kingdom on top of them. Being in Florida, a basement was all but impossible. You dig down two feet here and you hit water.

"Anyway, these tunnels run across the entire park. They allow the cast members to get from point A to point B directly, without having to navigate massive crowds."

They descended and started through the tunnels. The walls were color-coded and bore the name of the land above them.

Dozens of cast members passed in all directions. Suddenly Mickey Mouse appeared out of a side room and started up a set of stairs.

"Hey, I asked to talk to him," Eric called ahead to Victor.

"I thought you wanted to talk to the person you interacted with yesterday?" Victor asked as he looked back at him.

It never occurred to him that there would be more than one Mickey.

"How many are there?" he asked.

"Well if you mean cast members, we normally have three on site on any given day. If you mean total people who are trained to be Mickey … a few dozen at least. Funny thing is there are almost as many versions, too. We have a Mickey for every occasion. There are dozens of different outfits."

He didn't even know what to think of that. He'd gotten a part-time job when he was in college, at a place that had a mascot. He'd never done it himself, but he knew that there were only two people willing to do it, and there was only one costume to be shared. He was grateful he'd never had to climb into that thing. From what his co-workers told him, it was hot and smelly. He didn't know how Disney found so many people who were happy to do it.

He soon found himself completely disoriented. The tunnels seemed to go on forever. Other than the changing colors and names on the walls, everything looked the same. It seemed like they had walked miles, but he knew it couldn't have been that far.

They finally stopped at another run-of-the-mill door. Victor held an RFID reader up to the receiver and a loud click emanated from the door. They pushed through into a fairly bland room with a table and chairs in the middle. In the corner was a fridge and a couple of vending machines. One wall had a couch up against it. The final feature was a TV mounted on a wall across from the couch.

"This is the command center?" Eric asked, looking around.

"Part of it. Think of this as our green room," Victor said with a smile as he walked over to the vending machines. He swiped his reader in front the panel and then punched in his choice.

Eric expected a snack to fall down. Instead, the vending machine swung open, revealing a portal. The voices and the sound of computers floated out.

He followed Victor into a room that looked like something out of a movie. One wall was comprised entirely of monitors. Instead of just video feeds, there were real-time statistics floating across many of them.

There were more than ten workstations. Each one had dual monitors with video feeds and a mail console. Seated at each workstation was a cast member wearing a headset. Instead of using a mouse, they simply waived their hands and pointed.

He had heard Microsoft was working on Kinect for Windows, but he hadn't seen it in action. When he looked closer, however, he realized the workstations did not appear to be running Windows.

"What are they using? A Windows overlay?" he asked as he turned toward Victor.

"No. It's our own proprietary version of Linux. We can focus far more of the computer's' resources on processing when we don't have a myriad of crap running in the background," Victor said with a wicked grin.

"From here they can pull up nearly any spot in the park, minus the restrooms. Our employees also filter through hits that the computers generate. Before you even ask, it's not facial recognition or anything like that. That would be tedious and a waste of time. To be honest, we don't care if a criminal is in the parks, as long as he keeps his nose clean. The computer was programmed to pick up on people moving differently."

"Ninety-nine percent of people fall into one mold or another. The ones that don't are often executing "unnatural" movements. Such as bending and twisting in a way that a person wouldn't do by accident. Most of those people are doing one of two things: stealing or abusing drugs or alcohol."

"Afraid they are going to cut into your liquor sales?" Eric jokingly asked.

"No. It wasn't until the "Be Our Guest" restaurant opened up that we even offered alcohol in the Magic Kingdom. Anyway, we don't worry so much about alcohol, unless someone appears aggressive or heavily intoxicated."

"We're almost done compiling all of the footage on the victim. It should be ready for you in a couple of hours."

Eric scrunched up his face and asked, "What's taking so long?"

"We have eight hours of footage for you," Victor responded.

Eric had lost track of how many times his mind had been blown in the last two days. He knew what he was going to be doing tonight, and most likely for the entire night. There went his hope of catching up on sleep.

Changing the subject, he asked, "Did your computer catch me yesterday? Is that why the cast member approached me and asked me if I had multiple cell phones?"

Victor grinned before responding, "No. We really do train our people to look for body language and odd stuff. We don't just rely on the computer. The multiple layers give us a big edge. There is a reason we've never been bombed. It's not for lack of trying."

"How do you keep that secret?"

"People are fairly predictable. When we see someone who is up to something illicit, we make a scene. We cry out that the person just won a seven-day cruise on the Disney Cruise Line. We ask them to follow us to pick up the voucher and fill out some paperwork. We take them into the Utilidors and then kick the crap out of them."

Eric thought about that for a moment. Since Disney was its own entity, they technically could make their own laws. In fact, the Orange County Sheriff's Department wasn't allowed onto Disney property until a few years earlier. Disney only allowed them in because they didn't want to mess with ticketing people. They'd rather have someone else ruin the day for one of their guests.

Victor continued, "In the case of a suicide bomber, we tranquilize them. We use a horse tranquilizer that can knock out a 200 pound man in less than a minute. A specially trained security cast member accidentally bumps into them; the needle is so small most people don't feel it."

"How often does a suicide bomber show up?" Eric asked as he tried to keep the wonder out of his voice.

"After 9/11 we intercepted ten the first year. Within three

years, the total was down to about three a year. We haven't had one in the last two years. Nothing discourages like failure," Victor explained.

"I'm amazed they haven't hit Universal or Sea World," Eric said as he crossed his arms.

"They are our rivals when it comes to drawing crowds. We've tech-shared with them on the security side. If any of us get attacked, it would severely impact the entire area," Victor said with a mirthless smirk.

Eric looked back at Victor and asked, "What about the RFID readers. Who can I talk to about that?"

Victor nodded and said, "I should be able to answer any questions you have about them. Let's go back to the green room. It'll be more comfortable in there."

He followed Victor back into the green room and then took a seat at the table. Victor walked over to the fridge and opened it.

"Would you like something to drink?" Victor asked as he opened the refrigerator door.

He jokingly replied, "Make mine a Moxie!"

Victor stepped away from the fridge holding two Moxies.

Eric just gawked and said, "Are you kidding me!?! I haven't seen Moxie in years. Why on Earth would Disney stock that?"

Victor laughed and explained, "I'm originally from Maine. I know I can stock this in a shared fridge and not worry about anyone taking one. Well, maybe one, but they definitely won't take a second!"

That made him laugh. He knew Victor wasn't kidding. Moxie tasted like someone dumped coffee, cough medicine, root beer, and molasses into a bottle and then carbonated it.

He had found few things as polarizing. You either loved it or hated it. There was no middle ground when it came to Moxie. He had found that out in college when he used to trick his friends into trying the stuff. Some of them had actually spit it out. Of the dozens he tricked into trying it, only two had ended up liking it.

"Why don't I start by telling you how the readers function? That might be faster," Victor said as he sat down across from him.

"The reader only has one tiny bit of data in it; a single unique number. The corresponding readers in the parks are connected to a database. Some are hardwired, but a few are wireless. The wireless ones are minimal because they cost ten times what the hardwired ones do. The reason they are so expensive is because they are 128-bit encrypted with our own homegrown algorithm. In other words, they are impossible to hack."

"What kind of information is accessed?" Eric asked as he sat back in his chair.

"Everything in our reservation system, which also ties into the ADR and Fastpass system, can be accessed. So there is a good chunk of private data. You may have noticed when you checked in, that we asked for some personal information, that people normally don't question," Victor said as he took a sip of his soda.

"Like how the cast member slyly asked if any of us were celebrating anything or how many times we'd been to Disney," Eric stated.

Victor nodded and said, "We can register that data for each sub account on the reservation. Each sub account gets its own band. That way no one is left out and everyone gets a personalized experience."

He took a swig of his Moxie and then said, "That takes care of readers. Now I just need to meet the mouse. You said he was around right?"

Victor gave him a look that made him feel like he had missed something he should have caught.

When the Head Comes Off

"You have good timing. The cast member you ran into yesterday just finished up the afternoon parade. Everyone has shifted so it should only be a couple of minutes," Victor said as he looked down at his smartphone to confirm his information.

"Shifted? What do you mean?" Eric asked.

Victor looked up and explained, "We have to make sure the parade float is well out of sight before Mickey shows up again at the meet and greet location. That way Mickey never appears in two places at the same time in the same park. Just imagine if a kid met Mickey only to walk outside the building and see him on a float. That would ruin the magic wouldn't it?"

"I have some other things I have to attend to. You have my contact information right?"

Eric nodded to Victor and watched him leave the room. He pulled out his phone to check his messages. He realized he had no signal. He should have known better. He might as well be in a bomb shelter.

The door beeped and Mickey Mouse walked in.

The site was so surreal that it put him into a goofy mood. He wasn't sure if it was the lack of sleep or information overload but he decided to be a wise guy.

"Ah! Mr. Mouse, thank you for joining me. I'd like to ask you a few questions. Just us, man to man."

Mickey reached up and slightly twisted his head. He smiled because he half expected to hear air escape, like a spaceman in a movie. The smile fell off his face when Mickey pushed up and removed the head.

"How about woman to wiseass? Will that work?"

He couldn't talk. He was so astonished he just couldn't respond. Before him sat an incredibly cute, petite blonde girl who appeared to be in her early twenties. She wasn't beautiful like a supermodel, but the kind of cute that was ten times as attractive in his eyes. Her blonde hair was so light it was almost white and was cut short in a kind of bob. She had the longest part of her hair tucked behind her ears. Her eyes were a shocking shade of brown. They were so light they almost seemed to glow. After a second he decided that they were an odd shade of amber.

Despite her attractiveness, what really threw him off his guard was her smile. When she smiled it was almost a physical force, knocking him back a step and inexplicably making him blush. It took him a minute to figure that it was because she pulled off that dangerous, naughty look that drew men like a moth to a flame.

"Mouse got your tongue?" She asked as she covered her mouth to hide a laugh.

It was then that he realized that he'd been silent since she sat down. He quickly stammered out, "I just have a few questions about what you do."

She gave him a funny look and responded, "Okay … most of the time people start with, 'Hello my name is … Nice to meet you.'"

He could feel the blood flushing up into his face. He looked down in embarrassment and said, "Detective Eric Highland."

She sighed as she leaned forward and picked up his hand off the table, and then started to shake it.

"I'm Sasha Cole. It's nice to meet you," she said with a touch of sarcasm in her voice.

Now he was truly embarrassed. He couldn't even look at her anymore. He felt like a rookie who had never interviewed anyone. He knew that if Jose had been in the room, he would have been curled up in the corner, laughing so hard he wouldn't be able to speak.

He had never been a ladies' man, but he never acted like this. He knew he should be professional and pull it together, but Sasha so enamored him, it left a pit in his stomach. It was that awful feeling you got when you knew you were attracted to someone, but also knew you didn't have a chance with them.

"Does it have to be now? I just got done with the parade. If you couldn't tell, I'm soaked in sweat. There may be a fan in the head and a liquid cooling vest but it still gets very hot in this thing."

"It's not as bad at the meet and greets, because those are air conditioned, but the parades are brutal. You move around five times as much, and you're under the blazing sun."

He didn't look up. He just couldn't muster the strength. All he could do was say, "We can do this after you take a shower or something."

She leaned forward and said, "I have a better idea. How about you buy me dinner tomorrow night and I'll tell you everything you want to know?"

Her blunt offer almost blew him out of his seat. It certainly rendered him speechless.

"Yes I am asking you out. You're handsome, in shape, don't work for Disney, and best of all, you're not from around here. If you are, I'm not sure how you picked up a New York accent," she said as she cocked her head to the side.

That broke the spell and allowed him to respond, "I'm not from New York! I'm from Boston!"

She grinned and said, "I know. My grandmother was

originally from Boston. If I had ever told her she was from New York, she would have tanned my hide, but I figured that would at least get you to look me."

"So what time should I pick you up?" she asked.

"I can pick you up," he quickly offered.

"No. What if you turn out to be bad news? I don't want you knowing where I live," she said as her grin only widened.

"I could meet you somewhere."

She shook her head and said, "That's just wasteful. If you are buying me dinner I can at least drive. What, are you afraid of having a 105-pound girl knowing where you live?"

He knew she was goading him, but he couldn't help but respond, "Six o'clock."

Head-butting

Eric walked into the conference room and wanted to turn right around and walk out. The tension in the room was intense. Seated around the table were Jose, Captain Hunter, Fidel "El Guapo," their lead forensic tech Dr. Riko Matsuzaka, and Victor Webb from Disney.

"Good, we are all here, so we can get started," Captain Hunter barked out. "Let's begin with what we know. Javon's parents left the room at 10:15 and arrived back around 10:30 to find his body. Ortega, give us a quick overview of the concrete evidence we have."

He could tell by looking at Jose that something was bothering him.

Jose sat back in his chair and read off a series of bullet points to the group:

- The door was unlocked at 10:21 by the father's bracelet.

- Only the mother was seen on the video footage, where the soda fountains were.

- The only fingerprints found at the scene belonged to the family and the cast members who had serviced the room.

- The victim had approached the murderer.

- There was no sign of a struggle.

He leaned forward in his chair asked Victor, "You were able to give me eight hours of footage on the family. Very little of it was from the resort. Why is that?"

Victor shrugged his shoulders and explained, "The resorts are not major targets so we only have cameras in sensitive areas."

Captain Hunter looked around and then yelled out, "Theories!"

Victor was the first to respond, "We have a camera on part of the walkway from the building they were in, to the Great Ceremonial House. We saw them walking toward the G.C.H. and we saw them walking back around 10:28. There is a side path just beyond the view of the camera that follows the building around to the other two doors. It sounds like the father ran up the path and back into the building."

Eric shook his head, "According to my information, this was their first time visiting Disney World. It was also their first day. How would he have known where the cameras were? Not only that, why wouldn't he have just left the door open cracked open? Using your key is a huge mistake."

"No one said he was smart," Captain Hunter spat out.

"Actually, we do know that he's smart," Jose said as he turned toward the captain.

"He graduated from Ohio State on the dean's list. He made it on a full scholarship, which he obtained because of his academic accomplishments in high school. Starting with nothing, he bought a struggling used car dealership, turned it around, and used it as a launching pad. He now owns five large, very successful dealerships in the Chicago area."

Eric could tell the Captain was starting to get steamed. He wanted this to be an open and shut case.

"That doesn't mean he didn't make mistakes!" Reggie boomed.

Eric tried to draw some of the heat away from Jose by saying, "We are also missing the murder weapon. They didn't throw it in the trash or the lake. They also didn't dump it in a bush or leave it in the room. If we want to nail down the killer, we need that razor."

Dr. Matsuzaka piped up and said, "If you find it, I can match it. Blades leave distinct marks. All of them have imperfections we can match up. Thankfully, the victim was not stabbed. Those wounds are much more difficult to match exactly."

Victor spoke next and unknowingly set off the Captain Reginald Hunter bomb, "Hey, if you have a motive do you really need the murder weapon?"

"Why don't you just sit there and be silent unless we ask

you a question!" Hunter exploded.

Jose looked over at Victor with an apologetic look and explained, "We don't have a motive. There was no insurance policy. Even if there was, the family is independently wealthy. There was no history of abuse and no evidence of such on the mother or child. No history of mental illness. There was also nothing on the video footage to imply a strained relationship. We have nothing."

"We don't need a motive! The father has no alibi for the timeframe beyond the mother's word, and he opened the door," Hunter coolly relayed.

Eric was nervous now. His recreation of Javon's last day had absolutely convinced him that the parents were not involved. He knew he couldn't just say he had a feeling, so he decided to take a different approach, "Captain, you realize that if you are right, we will be making two arrests. If the mother is involved, she is one amazing actress."

Before the Captain could respond Jose chimed in, "Detective Highland is right. Everything about her demeanor was inconsistent with someone who had just been involved in a murder, never mind the murder of her own child."

"Body language doesn't trick juries and it doesn't change facts," Hunter said coldly.

Eric leaned forward and looked at Victor. "I just thought of something. Is there a master account for the room?"

Victor cocked an eyebrow and asked, "You mean on the booking?"

"Yes."

"Yes, there always is. The booking is made under one person and all the other guests are placed under it."

"So, if you were going to duplicate one of the of RFIDs, it would be that one."

"You think a cast member is the killer?" Jose carefully asked.

Eric shook his head and said, "I don't know, but we can't rule it out. I don't think we have enough information to rule anything out."

Reggie slapped the desk and said, "To hell with that idea! Let's go around the table. Majority wins. I'm a yes for the father."

Next they went to Victor. After a moment he nodded for the father. Eric and Jose both emphatically said no. Dr. Matsuzaka had to abstain in case she was called to the stand. That left El Guapo.

Eric felt bad. He could tell by looking at El Guapo that he didn't want to say yes. The guy was sweating bullets. On one hand, if he said no he'd have to deal with the captain's rage. If he said yes, he'd be voting against what he believed.

It occurred to him that the Captain did this on purpose. Normally the Captain was easy to work with. He was an overall decent guy. The stress of this case had gotten to him.

The captain stared right through poor Fidel. Finally the man bowed his head and just nodded.

Knowing he was defeated, Jose quickly defused the situation, offering a recommendation, "The parents are still in the area. They are not a flight risk. Let's take our time and do this right. Jumping the gun on this will only hurt us. Let's get our ducks in a row and make the arrests tomorrow. I think we all can agree we want this to be as clean as possible."

Everyone nodded in agreement.

Eric looked up at Jose and saw his own feelings reflected. This was wrong.

Coffee

Eric sat in the chair across from Jose's desk. They both had giant cups of coffee in their hands but neither was interested in drinking. They felt defeated, but there was nothing they could do.

"I can understand why Reggie was so insistent. He got a call from the governor yesterday," Jose offered as he stared down at his desk.

Eric looked up in surprise, "The governor called after less than two days?"

For a moment he thought it was Buddy sitting in front of him when Jose said "It's Disney."

"Did you find anything on your walk-through that stood out?" Jose asked trying to keep the hope out of his voice.

"No. I even watched eight hours of video footage last night to see if the Jones' experience differed from my own. It was shockingly similar. It was so close, it was almost to the minute. That touring plan they used really did direct you around the crowds and bottlenecks."

"All that walk-through did was convince me that the parents didn't do it."

Jose just shook his head and said, "Thank God it's Thursday. Are you going to be there at the usual time?"

Eric cursed himself. He forgot to let Jose know he couldn't make it to their gym night. Every Thursday Jose kicked the crap out of him on his crazy obstacles. Afterward, he kicked the crap out of Jose by swimming laps around him in the pool. Then they destroyed themselves at Spanky's, an awful dive bar with cheap booze and fried food. After all, what fun was pushing yourself so hard in the gym if you didn't completely counter any and all of the benefits after?

"Sorry, I can't make it," he said uncomfortably.

"Say what?" Jose exclaimed as gave him the stink eye.

"What are you hiding? And don't even think about saying nothing, because I can tell by the way your shoulders are slumped and how you're looking all around that you are hiding something."

Eric kept his head down and said, "I've got a date."

Jose gave him an incredulous look for a moment and then blurted out, "Holy crap, you're not kidding!"

Eric just nodded and cursed himself again. He could feel the blood rushing to his face. Jose was going to have a field day with this.

"Well … Hell, I'm going to mark the calendar! I've known you for five years and the only girls I've ever seen you around were the ones someone set you up with. I was starting to think you liked guys more than girls."

Eric frowned at that and shot back, "Maybe I do. Then what would you do?"

His dig failed. Jose easily picked up on the fact that Eric was kidding, but he took it seriously and said, "I'd stand up, give you a big hug, and congratulate you for finally coming out of the closet! I know some nice guys who would love to meet someone like you, if you want me to hook you up."

After a moment Jose's smile faded and he said, "But seriously, who are you going out with?"

Eric couldn't keep a straight face as he honestly said, "Mickey Mouse."

The Date

Eric was sweating bullets. He couldn't remember the last time he was this nervous. He ran over to the mirror to double check that his tie was straight and his shirt looked clean. Looking down at his black slacks, he hoped they were ok.

He started to pace around his small home, looking at his watch. He still had another ten minutes before she was supposed to arrive; thirty before he could say she blew him off, but he knew that wasn't going to happen. She didn't know the investigation was over. She had to show up or risk having him question her at her work.

He nearly jumped out of his skin when the doorbell rang. He took a deep breath to steady himself and headed over to the door. It felt like someone had forced a stupid pill down his throat, because he forgot about his training as a cop. He didn't even look through the peephole. That was something he always he did before opening the door. It was a habit that came naturally after years of working crime scenes.

He swung the door open and there she was. Under his breath he cursed himself.

She was wearing khaki Capri pants and a pink camisole. She had fashionable sandals on her feet that allowed her painted toenails to show. Her hair was pinned back to the side by a barrette.

"Where did you think we were going?" she asked as she looked him up and down.

"I ummm …"

"I really must have impressed you," she said as she gave him an utterly evil smile.

He tried to compose himself, but he was too late, and he felt his face flush.

"Awww, you're blushing. That's so cute."

The last thing he wanted to be was "cute." He just hung his head and muttered, "Give me a minute to change."

As he turned around and headed for his bedroom he heard her call out, "If you change your pants make sure they make your butt look as good as those do."

She followed that up with a cheerful giggle.

Ten minutes later he was in his normal comfortable dress. As he walked out the door, he caught a whiff of Sasha's perfume. He had no idea what it was, but for some reason it made his pulse race. How was he going to survive the entire date? He already felt dizzy.

He turned and saw Sasha's car sitting in his driveway. His first thought was: How had it made it more than a mile without crapping out? His second thought was: How had this thing made it past inspection?

"Do you like my crap box?" Sasha asked with a big grin.

He couldn't help but think that "crap box" was a fitting description.

"How old is this thing?" he asked.

"It's a '98 Nissan Altima with 223,000 miles on it. I told myself years ago that I was going to drive this thing till it died. I thought that would be a year or two back then."

She turned toward the car and said, "It runs and it has AC. Considering my income, I can't ask for much more."

"Come on," she said as she grabbed his hand and pulled him toward the car.

He got in the passenger seat and shut the door. It popped open. He tried again. It popped open again.

"You have to really slam it. The latch isn't that great," she explained.

He slammed the door and it finally held. He quickly put on his seat belt and made sure it was secure. He had no faith that the door would stay shut after they got going.

"Oh, do me a favor and don't put the window down. It doesn't go back up. At least not easily."

She turned the key and the engine sputtered, but didn't take. She just looked at Eric and smiled as she tried it again. The engine kicked in and the whole car shook for a second.

She smiled again and said, "There we go!"

She pulled out what looked like a 1st gen iPod that had been bedazzled. She caught him staring at it and said, "Hey it works."

She plugged the iPod into an old school tape deck adapter that people used to play CDs in their car when they didn't have a CD player.

"The radio doesn't work, but the tape deck runs, so I can still play tunes. Do you like Kate Nash?" she asked looking up at him.

"I don't know. I can't say I've ever heard of her," he said as he shrugged his shoulders.

"It seems like no one in the states knows who she is. She's a British singer/songwriter. Her first two CDs were good, but I really like this third one. However, if you don't like punk you'll probably hate it."

"I don't mind punk," he told her, and he wasn't just being nice. When he was growing up, Boston had a thriving hardcore scene. He had picked up a taste for the music after going to a few shows with his friends.

It wasn't until years later that he came to understand he'd been in the middle of a hardcore renaissance. Some of the bands he had seen had gone on to become underground legends. One of the shows he went to was still talked about to this day. He was just a kid, but had managed to get into the basement of the Middle East across the river in Cambridge. They didn't even try to stop him at the door. They just took his money and waved him through.

That show became legendary because of the lineup. The mix was just bizarre. The show started off with Boston's own *Blood for Blood*. They had drawn their normal crowd. A lot of their crowd was in a "crew" together. If you asked the Feds they were a local gang.

After *Blood for Blood*, *Marauder* took the stage. They drew a mixed bag of general hardcore fans, but they also tended to pull in a lot of metal fans too.

Those two bands wouldn't have been a strange mix on their own, but the next band pushed it over the edge. The legendary *Madball* took the stage next. *Madball* was out of NYC and a lot of fans came with them. It was a cop's nightmare. A lot of *Madball's* fans were in a "crew" too. On paper there should have been bloodshed, but the two gangs were not rivals, and were actually friendly. Neither was violent unless provoked.

The cherry on top of the sundae was the headliner. *Earth Crisis* drew a ton of vegan, straightedge kids from miles and miles away. Rarely did that crowd mix with the non-straightedge crowd, but on that night, the stars seemed to align, and one of the most epic shows of all time went down without a hitch.

Sasha pulled out of the driveway and sped off down the road. As she drove she sang along with the music, bobbing her head back and forth. He couldn't help but laugh. Instead of being offended she smiled and sang louder.

As it turned out, only a few of the songs were really punk. There was a nice mix, if not an odd one. Some song called 3AM burned into his head and would not go away.

It finally occurred to him that he should at least find out where they were going.

"So, are we going far?"

She shook her head and said, "No. We're headed to Downtown Disney. Since you're paying, we're hitting one of my favorite places."

He wasn't really worried when she said that. If they had been dressed up it might have been cause for concern. How much damage could you do dressed like this?

Car Bomb

They pulled into one of the Downtown Disney parking lots and, incredibly, found an empty spot right away. After getting out of the car, Sasha walked over to Eric and grabbed his hand with a smile.

"Follow me, Detective Highland," she said with a naughty look on her face.

They walked through a good chunk of Downtown Disney. He was very grateful they did not stop at a place called the T-Rex. It looked like a tourist trap and sounded loud enough to give anyone a migraine.

They finally stopped at a place called Raglan Road.

She turned to him and explained, "I love this place. I figured you'd like it too, since you're from Boston."

When they entered the front door, he quickly realized that she was not wrong. The place felt like something you'd find in Boston. All the smallest details merged together to give the impression that you were in a real Irish pub.

They were seated at a table near a small stage.

"Some nights they have live entertainment. We're too early to see anything tonight. We'll be gone long before anything starts," she said with a shrug.

It occurred to him that he might have chosen a time that was a little early for most dates. He suddenly felt like an old man.

"What can I get you guys?" asked a large waiter with a big black beard and an Irish accent.

Eric spoke up first and asked, "Can I get a black and tan, but can I swap out the Bass Ale?"

The waiter gave him a stern look before replying, "Yes, but if you ask me to swap it out with Bud or Bud Light I might have to punch you in the face."

He laughed and shook his head, "New Castle."

The waiter perked up and nodded his approval. "Good choice. I might have to try that later. Never made a black and tan with New Castle."

The waiter turned to Sasha and asked what she would like. He expected her to say a wine cooler or some kind of martini. He nearly wet himself when he heard her response.

"Irish Car Bomb please!"

She must have noticed the stunned looking on his face because she said, "I'm only having one drink but I'm definitely going to make it count!"

A few minutes later their drinks arrived. Apparently the

waiter told his co-workers because a handful of people showed up to see the little blonde girl take on a car bomb.

Sasha dropped the shot of Bailey's into the pint of Guinness and started to chug. Everyone began to cheer her on. He even joined in at the end. She finished the drink and slammed down her mug. A cheer went up which turned to a roar of laughter when she let out a huge belch.

She turned beet red and meekly said, "Excuse me."

After a few minutes of chitchat, she leaned back in her chair and said, "So what did you want to know about being the Mouse?"

He looked her in the eye and said, "For starters, what's it like being Mickey?"

She thought for a minute and said, "It's pretty decent. You get to ham it up sometimes. Some groups are better than others. Being in Florida you get some really stinky people and that sucks."

She took a sip of water and continued, "I've been doing it for about a year now. It hasn't gotten old yet, which is nice. Plus it's good therapy."

He could tell right away that the last thing slipped out. Her eyes got wide and she looked down. He knew she was praying he hadn't taken note of what she said.

He couldn't help himself. The cop inside of him overruled

the dating part of his head, which told him to drop it.

"Why is it good therapy?" he asked.

"Oh, hell," she said to herself as she looked up at the ceiling.

After a second she composed herself and said, "Okay. The shrink told me not to run from it, so I'm just going to lay it out there. I guess it's better that you find out up front so you can run while you have the chance."

She took a breath to compose herself and then started in, "When I was two, my parents were killed by a drunk driver. I was sent to live with my grandmother in Boise, Idaho. She died when I was eight years old. I was then shipped off to a boarding school.

"Most of the kids at the school were from elite, crazy rich families. To "serve the community" the school took in a certain amount of misfits and orphans like me.

"After only a week, a group of boys my age started to … take advantage of me. They were a bunch of entitled brats who thought they could do anything they wanted because their parents had money.

"For five years I tried to ignore what was happening. I pretended that if I didn't think about what was happening, it wasn't real. When I turned 13, I lost control. One day I grabbed a baseball bat and put two of them in the hospital.

It was then that the authorities found out what had been happening to me.

"It took five years of therapy for me to be able to interact with boys in a civil manner. I tried to move on with my life. I went to school at Oregon State but almost flunked out my first year. I was ok around guys, but when kids were around I'd almost breakdown. I ended up going back to therapy.

"After I graduated, I knew that if I was going to be able to deal with what happened, I had to grab it by the horns."

He looked at her as kindly as he could and said, "You got a job as a character."

She nodded and said, "Yeah. The mask let me hide my fear in the beginning."

"How did you end up in Disney World? Wasn't Disneyland a lot closer?"

"Two months before she died, my grandmother brought me here. It's the best memory I have. It was ..."

He could see tears welling in her eyes as her voice cracked. He thought about a few days earlier and his own experience tromping through the Magic Kingdom, with his friends. He reached out and took her hand. When she looked up he just nodded and squeezed her hand.

Back to Business

Sasha excused herself for a moment to go to the restroom. When she returned she explained that the whole pub had been imported from Ireland. It was a true recreation except for one thing.

He looked around. He couldn't see anything out of place. So he asked her, "What's the one thing?"

"The restroom isn't in the basement! In most pubs in Ireland and the U.K. you have to walk down a nasty flight of stairs to get to the restroom. I swear it's how they determine when to cut people off. If you can't make it down the stairs and back up, you can't have another drink."

She shook her head for a second and said, "Sorry I got off track. I'm sure you wanted to know about what I do, unless you goal was to trick me into a date."

"Wait a minute, you asked me out," he started to protest.

"Semantics, semantics," she said laughing.

"Ok then, how does the voice trick work?" he asked trying to get serious again.

"Ah, a lot of my friends ask me that. It's a secret, that only the cast members who are trained on a character like that, know.

"In your non-dominate hand you have pressure sensitive triggers in each finger on the glove. You press your finger to your thumb to trigger them. They are the four most popular inquires or statements we run into. I don't even know how much research it took to figure them out.

"My index finger is the 'happy' finger." Sasha paused a moment for effect before continuing, "If I see a birthday pin or another similar pin on someone, I press that finger. Before it responds, it pings the reservation system to see who is celebrating what.

"My middle finger is my generic 'Magical Day' finger. It determines who is closest and says their name.

"My ring finger is the resort trigger. That's the one that seems to go the extra mile with people and adds a sense of realism.

"My pinky finger is my emergency finger. I push that if a kid is crying. When I hit it, it says 'Will you be my friend?' You'd be amazed how often that works."

Eric just scratched his head. It seemed like they had thought of everything.

He decided he'd had enough of work and was determined to change the subject.

"The Ducks are better than the Beavers," he said very seriously.

Her eyes went wide and he was afraid she was going to jump across the table and choke him. "In your dreams, you wannabe security guard!" she spat back at him.

His laugh gave away the ruse. She caught on and said, "I was wondering why you would have even cared. I was about to tell you that the Red Sox weren't a fart in the wind compared to the Yankees."

He stopped laughing and said, "It's a good thing you didn't."

This time she started laughing.

"Anyway that's 90% of the enjoyment of college and sports. I don't like sports for what they are, but I can really get into the rivalry," she said as she looked him in the eye. She then asked, "What about you, where did you go to school?"

"The University of New Hampshire."

"Yuck! Sounds like a redneck festival."

"You couldn't be any farther from the truth. New Hampshire may be a small state, but it packs a big bang for the buck. I met a lot of great people when I was there. I think the cold winters do something to the people. It converts them to the salt of the Earth. Granted, there were some pricks, but mostly it was an awesome experience. Plus there were the hockey games."

Sasha perked up and nearly shot out of her seat. "You like

hockey!?!"

"Yes. The northeast is hockey central. UNH was almost always in the top ten in the country when I was there. There were so many rivalries you could barely count them all, but nothing quite matched up to the big two: UNH vs. UMaine and BC vs. BU. Those two were something to see."

Sasha responded, "I can't believe you like hockey. No one down here likes hockey. I try to talk to people about hockey and they look at me like I'm a few sandwiches short of a picnic."

"My favorite team is …"

He quickly interrupted, "Don't you dare say the Montreal Canadiens! If you do I'm leaving!"

She gave him a sinister grin and then said, "No, I grew up in Idaho. It's Vancouver. And, by the way, we still owe you for beating us back in 2011. I'm assuming you are a Bruins fan, based on your Canadiens comment."

He nodded. He wasn't sure if it was the beer, but he felt warm inside. It had been a long time since he had connected with someone like this. He just hoped he didn't screw it up.

The End

They chatted for the rest of the dinner and all the way back to Eric's house. They found themselves laughing more often than not. At times they were laughing so hard they drew stares from the people around them. At one point on the way home he said something that made Sasha laugh so hard he had to grab the wheel so they didn't run off the road.

They even shared dumb things they would never have told anyone else. He admitted that he could recite almost word for word the entire script to the *Goonies*. He and a friend used to watch it every Friday, when his friend slept over.

When she heard that story, she cried out, "Wooooo! Velveeta and a good time!"

He looked at her for a moment. That certainly wasn't a term he'd ever heard.

She saw his perplexed look and said, "Every Friday at the boarding school they use to serve Velveeta. That might not sound like a big deal but compared to the slop they normally served, it was a delicacy. After that it was movie night. Some of us came up with that cheer when something good happened."

He didn't mean to, but he burst out laughing again. It must have been infectious because she soon followed and they nearly ran off the road again.

They made it back to his house in one piece.

When they arrived, she popped out of the car. When he got out he was waiting for him. She grabbed him and kissed him hard on the lips. It wasn't an overly romantic kiss. It was just hard and intense. He half expected to hear a popping noise when she pulled away.

"Here's my cell phone, email, and Facebook. It's better to text me or email me. I have a prepaid phone that only has minimal minutes on it, but I get free texts. When you Facebook me we can set up our second date."

He was stunned by her blunt manner but realized he had no desire to argue. He took her info and put it in his pocket.

"Wow, look at the time! 7:30! If I'm fast I might be able to catch the early bird special at the Asian Super Buffet over on Route 50," she said sarcastically.

"I'll plan better next time," he said apologetically.

"No, this was good. It was nice and safe. If you had turned out to be a grumpy old fart I could have easily escaped after I broke your hip!"

"How do you know I'm not really a grumpy old fart who was just faking it the whole time?" he asked her with his best sly grin.

"Well if that's the case, I better pack my pepper spray next time!"

"Better not. Part of the training to be a cop is getting hit with a Taser and being nailed with pepper spray. The pepper spray was a hundred times worse."

She put on an inquisitive look for a moment before saying, "Good to know. I'll have to get a bigger can."

Wake Up Call

Eric's phone went off at 11:30 p.m.. He cursed to himself as he looked to see who it was. It was Jose. Now Eric was just annoyed. They hadn't even made the arrest yet. The other crews should have been able to handle any additional homicides. Then again, they were making an arrest tomorrow. The paperwork was lined up and ready to go.

Still, it seemed like they were jumping the gun. When you were assigned a case, you worked that case only. The only exception was if you had a really simple, clear cut case, then they'd give you multiple ones. They had enough detectives to run three cases at a time without overlapping.

It occurred to him that he had been so focused on this case he wasn't aware what the workload for the other detectives was like.

Suddenly it hit him that he hadn't checked in with Jose after his date. This could easily be Jose's revenge for not filling him in.

He picked up his phone and swiped the screen to answer.

"What's up Jose?"

He was greeted with only silence. Suddenly his blood ran cold.

"Jose! Are you there man?!?"

He was starting to think that Jose had accidentally pocket-dialed him when he heard Jose clear his throat.

"Contemporary," was all he said.

He didn't understand.

"What's contemporary?"

What Jose said next made his heart jump into his throat.

"No, the Contemporary Resort. It happened again."

The Contemporary

Eric hadn't been paying attention any of the times he'd been close to the Contemporary. He stood next to his car and looked up at the hotel. It was much taller than any building at the Polynesian. From the outside it didn't seem very Disney. It just looked like an A-frame building. As he looked closer, he realized he was wrong and just shook his head. He'd forgotten about the Monorail.

The Monorail ran right through the middle of the hotel. He had ridden that monorail, even if he hadn't been paying attention at the time.

"Hi, Detective Highland."

He turned to see the same ginger-haired cast member that had greeted him at the Polynesian approaching.

"Buddy, don't you work at over at the Poly?" he asked him as he approached.

If he thought Buddy appeared nervous the previous night, he didn't have the words to describe how the kid looked now. The poor guy looked like he was about to break out in hives.

Buddy quickly nodded and almost stuttered as he said, "Yeah, but they decided to send me since I already knew you, and I have good knowledge of all of the resorts."

They started to walk toward the entrance. As they walked, he tried to calm down Buddy by getting him talking.

"It might help if you can tell me things the two resorts have in common."

Buddy perked right up. He hadn't expected to hear anything useful, but Buddy jumped right in.

"Both are original resorts that opened with the Magic Kingdom.

"Both were built by U.S. Steel. If you look up the side of the tower here you'll notice total uniformity. The reason for that is originally the rooms were put in place by a crane and then bolted into place. The idea was to unbolt them and swap them out when they needed to be updated. That didn't work out. The building settled a little and the rooms were warped into place.

"Both resorts are serviced by the Monorail and both of them have boat launches on the Seven Seas Lagoon.

"Both had notorious events take place at them. I told you about John Lennon breaking up the Beetles at the Poly. The Contemporary was the venue used to give one of the most famous political speeches of all time."

That caught him off guard. He looked at Buddy and asked, "Seriously? What speech was that?"

Buddy actually cracked a smile and said, "Nixon's 'I am not

a crook' speech. He was on vacation down here with his family and delivered the speech in one of the ballrooms."

While the information was interesting, the only thing he thought might be of any use was that they were both Monorail resorts.

They entered into the main lobby and he was underwhelmed. It was nice, but nothing like the Polynesian. This was just a lobby you'd find in a high-end hotel.

"They are working on the elevators right now. We can only take them from the fourth floor up, but there are escalators to take us there," Buddy explained as he power walked through the lobby.

As they went up the three floors, Eric was wondering why there was such a drastic difference in theming between the Poly and the Contemporary. So far everything had been nice, but why would anyone want to stay here over the Polynesian?

When they reached the top of the escalator at the fourth floor, his jaw dropped. They emerged into a massive open space. Arching up on both sides of the towering atrium were open halls with guest rooms. All around him were stores on the sides of the atrium and on the floor itself. He could see that on the far end was a restaurant.

On each end of the Atrium there were floor-to-ceiling glass walls with hatches where the monorail came in and out of the concourse. Near the middle was a massive pillar with an enormous mosaic scaling multiple floors.

"Impressive, isn't it?" Buddy asked as he looked back at Eric.

He just nodded his agreement as they headed toward the elevators.

When they got on the elevators and the doors swung shut, he noticed a nasty looking cut on Buddy's neck.

"What happened to your neck?" Eric asked as the elevator started up.

"Oh, I cut myself shaving," Buddy explained.

The cut looked a little too nasty to be a razor slip, but Eric let it drop.

Buddy turned nervously toward him and asked, "Um … if you're not busy tonight I'm having a party. It's just going to be some of my friends, but you'd be more than welcome."

Eric thought for a moment before turning to Buddy and nodding.

"You know what Buddy? That might be just what I need tonight."

Déjà Vu

Jose hadn't felt this awful in a long time. He looked across the room and felt sick. The air was beyond somber. Even El Guapo looked like someone had broken his spirit. Hardly anyone talked. Everyone just walked around like zombies doing their jobs.

The body was in almost the same place as the last one. A young Caucasian male between eight and 12 years old was on his back in a pool of his own blood. His throat had been slashed.

Jose took note of the blood spray. It was almost the same as the last victim. In fact, everything seemed identical. That's what made his blood run cold. So many things were similar, that it was easier for him to identify the things that were different, and those he could count on one hand.

He had never been on a crime scene where he felt like this. It didn't help when he looked at the corpse, either. Last time, the victim's hat had fallen off, which added to the violence of the scene. This time, his hat was still on. It wouldn't have been an issue if it was a beanie or baseball cap, but this was neither. The victim was wearing a modified ball cap. It had long black ears hanging off the sides and two fake teeth on the bill. It was designed to look like Goofy. It gave the scene a very disturbing feeling.

Normally, El Guapo made an announcement when Eric showed up on the scene. Not this time. He looked up to see Eric walk in the door. He saw the same mix of horror and disbelief wash over his partner when he spotted the victim. All of them had felt the same thing. He actually had to sit down for a moment to come to grips with his emotions.

He heard Eric say the same thing all of them had been thinking, "It's the same killer."

Jose quickly asked Eric, "What do you see?" His goal was not to find out any useful data, it was to try to kick Eric's mind into gear before he went into shock.

"My God, everything is the same. There is no way this is a copycat killer. We didn't release enough information to the public for anyone to duplicate this," Eric said as he shook his head.

"We know it wasn't Mr. Jones. He's been under surveillance. Plus, I'd bet anything that they are going to tell us it was a family member who opened the door," Jose chimed in.

Eric looked at him and said, "The press is going to go crazy with this."

Jose nodded and said, "I think the term 'hit the fan' is going to be an enormous understatement in this case."

"This be bad, very bad," El Guapo said from the corner.

No one could respond, so they all just nodded their agreement.

"Anyone need anything?" Jose looked up to see Victor Webb, who had been standing guard at the door.

"I was going to get some coffee and wasn't sure if you guys wanted anything."

Before anyone could answer, Victor's eyes went wide and he slapped his hand up to his ear.

"This is Victor. What did you just say?"

Jose stood up in time for Victor to look at him and Eric and say in a hushed voice, "One of my men spotted someone hiding in the bushes by one of the garden buildings."

The three of them shot through the door and ran down the hall at full speed.

The Chase

The group was outside in a matter of minutes. They slowed down as they approached the area where the person had been spotted. When they got close, a cast member waved them down.

"There is someone around the corner, on the left side, up against the building. I noticed him, but did not approach. I figured it was smarter to call it in and monitor the area," the cast member whispered.

Jose nodded his head and said, "Good job. What's the layout?"

Victor quickly chimed in, "It's a long path that leads down to the water. On the right side is some staging where they are doing work on the adjacent building."

Jose nodded and said, "Victor, take your man down and around to the far end and walk toward us. Belt out a loud laugh so we know you're in place. We'll start down the path and box him in."

Victor nodded and headed off with the cast member. Neither he nor Eric pulled their firearms. Instead, they pulled out their heavy duty flashlights. They wanted to take this guy down fast and clean. The last thing they needed was more bloodshed.

After a couple of minutes they heard Victor's laugh in the distance. They started down the path, a pace apart to make it extremely difficult for anyone to get by both of them.

He could sense slight movement in a bush off to the left. Instead of heading toward it he kept his pace steady. He'd break off at the last minute to give whoever was in the bush less time to react.

He could see Victor and the cast member off in the distance. He was going to motion to them to hold their ground when suddenly a small wiry man burst out of the bush. Instead of turning one way or another he made a beeline for the construction staging.

Time seemed to stand still. He burst into motion as he heard Eric cry out for the person to freeze. Victor and the cast member also jumped into action as they ran up the path.

The wiry man reached the staging. He jumped up, grabbed the lip and pulled himself up to the first platform. Like a cat, he ran down the planks and jumped to another section before climbing higher.

The perp may have thought he would easily out-climb most pursuers, but he hadn't counted on being chased by someone who trained on some of the most difficult obstacles in the world.

As Jose reached the staging, he heard Victor tell the cast member to run around to the other side.

Jose jumped up, caught a metal bar, and used his

momentum to snap himself up onto the wooden planks. As he did so, he heard Victor gasp in disbelief at the seemingly impossible leap.

By the time he had made it to the top of the staging, the man was only a few feet ahead. With a burst of speed, he easily overtook him. They crashed into gravel on the roof. After a brief struggle, he simply overpowered the small man.

Jose had the man on his feet and cuffed by the time Eric and Victor made it onto the roof.

"Let go of me you dirty Cube!" the man called out.

He just shoved him and told him, "I'm Mexican, not Cuban, but I'll make sure to send your regards to my Cuban buddies who work at the jail."

"Oh just great, a wetback, like that's any better!"

Before he could say anything, Eric cried out, "Shut your worthless mouth, you redneck piece of trash!"

In one swift motion Eric threw a brutal punch into the man's stomach. Jose heard the breath blow out of the man and saw him start to lurch forward. He timed it just right and raised his knee to intercept the man's face.

The man fell to his knees in a daze. Before anyone could move, Victor ran up and sprayed the man in the face with pepper spray.

Jose and Eric looked at Victor with shocked expressions.

"What? I saw him head-butt your knee. That's assault!"

Hangover

The high they had experienced in capturing the wiry man soon turned into disappointment. Instead of the killer, he was some lowlife Disney had been trying to find for a couple of months. He'd been breaking into unlocked cars and slipping into hotels to steal anything he could get his hands on. In the end, they attributed to him over $10k worth of stolen goods. He was a felon for sure, but not the killer.

Eric went home and crashed into his bed. He woke up at noon and for a moment wondered if it had only been a bad dream. He sat up and took a moment to come to terms with what he had seen earlier. No matter how he processed the data, he kept coming to one conclusion. The same person had killed both children.

He laid back down and rubbed his eyes. He prayed that they had caught the person on camera or that the killer had at least gotten sloppy. They needed something.

The fact that one person had killed twice was bad enough, but to have no evidence of that person from the first crime was crushing. It made him feel helpless. The revelation that someone had killed so cleanly made him sick to his stomach. What were the odds that someone who was so clean the first time would slip up?

His head was pounding. He felt like he was hung over. Thinking back, he realized he hadn't eaten anything since his date with Sasha last night. No wonder he had such a headache.

He got up and headed into the kitchen, hoping he had something that was still edible in the house. Opening the cabinet, he found a box of opened cereal that he couldn't even remember buying, and a loaf of bread that was more mold than anything else.

He opened the door to his fridge. There was a jug of milk that expired two months ago, some orange juice and a 12 pack of beer. When he opened the OJ, it hissed. He wasn't sure how long it took juice to ferment, so he couldn't guess how old it was. He looked at the beer, but decided that was an awful idea.

He shut the fridge door and opened the freezer. He smiled when he spotted a Publix frozen pizza. He grabbed the box and checked the date. To his delight, it hadn't expired yet. He threw it in the microwave and leaned against the wall.

As he waited, his mind wandered to his date with Sasha. Despite everything he'd been through since then, a smile spread across his face. That smile quickly faded. He had forgotten to friend her on Facebook. If she had figured out he had a profile, she might think he was blowing her off.

He forgot about the pizza and ran into his living room. He booted up his Mac. When it launched in seconds, he was truly glad he had spent the extra money to swap out the normal hard drive with a solid state drive. He just hoped he could remember his password. It took him five tries to get it right. He knew he should really go on more often. Matt and Sally were always posting stuff on his wall, and it also let him keep in touch with his mom.

He quickly punched in the Facebook address she had given him and breathed a sigh of relief when the page resolved. He added her as a friend and hoped he hadn't taken too long. After a few seconds, he decided it was best to follow it up with a text message.

"*Just added you as a friend,*" he texted to her. After a minute a text came back.

"*Bout time! What were u up to last night that u cdnt frnd me?*" she texted back.

"*M just bstn your chops. On BRK now. Kid barfed on me. Gettin new suit.*"

"*My stomach hurts. Laughed 2 hrd lst night.*"

"*G2G! TTYL XOXO*"

He knew exactly what she meant, because his stomach hurt, too. He hadn't laughed that hard in a long time. It wasn't often you got the chance to laugh so hard it hurt.

Within a minute, he received the notice that his friend request had been accepted. His detective instincts kicked in. He tried to fight them but he just couldn't muster the willpower to do so. It was time to check out her profile.

It always amazed him how much you could find out about someone by looking at their Facebook page. He often found that the things a person liked told you a lot more about them than their status updates. With that in mind, he navigated to Sash's "likes."

His impression of Sasha, based on their date, had been someone with a sense of humor, who said what was on her mind, whether it offended someone or not. His goal was to see if that was just a persona she had put on, or if she was really like that.

It was no persona. He found himself laughing out loud when he saw some of her likes. She had found some ridiculous pages and liked them.

He browsed through them and found:

People of Walmart

Stupid Facebook Pages

Oscar the Grouch

Raging Fat Kids

Drop Kicking Midgets

Lamebook

Park Wrecks

Everything else in her "likes" matched up with what he had expected.

He moved on to her photos. Normally, those were the second most helpful in seeing what a person was like. People often filtered their status updates but not their photos.

There were photos of her in her Mickey costume, with other cast members, in and around Disney World, and while she was out with friends. She seemed happy in all of them. She was amazingly photogenic. He hadn't seen a bad picture of her yet.

He moved on to her posts. She was blunt, sometimes with biting sarcasm. In one example, someone who appeared to be another cast member had posted some unwanted advances on her wall. At first she kindly turned him down. After telling him twice that she was not interested she unleashed her bluntness in full force.

She had posted "Are you really this stupid or did your mother drop you on your homely head as a child?"

There were no further posts from that cast member.

Suddenly, he felt guilty, and kind of like a creep. He told himself that this was public information and if she didn't want people to know it, she wouldn't have posted all of it. It didn't help.

He shut down his Mac and put his hands on his face. He felt frustrated and wound up, like he was going to explode. He needed to blow off some steam. Suddenly, he felt like bar hopping or going to a party.

If he was lucky they'd get the forensics by the end of the day. It all depended on how complex the evidence turned out to be. Sometimes it took days. Hr prayed that wouldn't be the case this time.

He sat up in his chair. There was a party he could go to. He whipped out his iPhone and called Buddy.

"Hello," a groggy voice on the other end answered. He felt bad. He had forgotten about Buddy's work schedule.

"Sorry Buddy, I didn't mean to wake you. I forgot you work nights," he apologized.

"Who is this?"

"It's Eric, Detective Highland."

"Oh, hey, what's going on?"

"Are you still having that party tonight?" he asked.

Buddy's voice perked right up and he said, "You bet! It's on like Donkey Kong!"

He shook his head and suppressed a laugh. Buddy was a

good kid but a total dork.

"Cool, count me in."

"Really!?! Awesome!"

"Is there anything you want me to bring?"

"No. We should be good. Thanks. I'll see you at six!"

He hung up the phone.

Six? What kind of a party started at six?

Deek Party

Eric pulled into the parking lot off RT 535. It looked like a run-of-the-mill apartment complex. He figured that's why the party was so early. Parties in apartment buildings normally ended with cops showing up due to a noise complaint.

He got out of his car and looked around. Something wasn't quite right. He took in the small details of the area and quickly determined that there were no children and all of the cars seemed to be run down or fairly inexpensive models. That didn't fit the surroundings.

The apartment complex was clean. No, it wasn't just clean, it was borderline spotless. Two things he rarely found side-by-side were poverty and cleanliness.

He checked the email he had gotten from Buddy to make sure he was in the right place and had the right building. This was the place all right.

He walked up to the door and pressed the buzzer.

"Hello?" came a female voice from the intercom.

He hadn't expected that. It was a party. You buzzed in anyone and everyone who showed up. That was half the fun of throwing a party.

He responded to intercom and said, "I'm here for the

party."

"Who are you?"

He wondered what kind of messed up party he was attending. Only the kinky ones vetted people at the door.

"I'm Eric. I know Buddy"

"Oh! You're real! We thought Buddy was kidding when he said he had a detective friend who was coming! You are a detective, right?"

He just stared at the intercom for a moment in disbelief before responding, "Yes, I am."

Finally, the door buzzed.

He walked up the stairs to the third floor. There was nothing but silence. He really started to get nervous. What was he walking into? At this point he hoped it was a dinner party. Buddy wasn't some kind of kinky weirdo was he? Sometimes it was almost impossible to tell, but he assumed that Buddy would have had the smarts to ask before inviting a stranger to some kind of sex party.

A door down the hall opened and Buddy's head popped out.

"Hey Eric, down here!" he cried out.

He could only see Buddy's head. He nearly turned and bolted for the exit. Somehow he composed himself and pressed forward. At this point, his curiosity had overwhelmed all the voices in his head screaming in alarm.

He walked through the door and looked around the room. He was greeted by more than a dozen smiling faces. The group was a total hodgepodge. African American, Asian, Latino, and Caucasian faces looked back at him. The age range appeared to be late teens to late sixties. Everyone was dressed conservatively.

"Oh my God!" he thought to himself in fear, "It's a cult!"

He almost jumped as heard the door shut behind him. The inquisition he went through at the door made sense now. His heart rate elevated as he realized he hadn't told anyone where he was going to be. He was grossly outnumbered. None of them looked like fighters, but you didn't have to be when you outnumber your opponent by more than ten to one.

"You picked a good night!" he heard Buddy say from behind him.

"We're watching *The Lion King* tonight."

He saw a number of people around the room nod in approval.

"Excuse me?" Eric asked.

"*The Lion King*, you know, the animated feature."

Buddy waved his hand across the room and explained, "These are my friends. We are a bunch of Deeks. Oh, that's a Disney geek.

"We get together every Friday for movie night. We've been working our way through the Disney catalog. Tonight is *The Lion King*."

Eric was so relieved he nearly collapsed. He started to laugh to himself.

"You don't like *The Lion King*?" Buddy asked meekly and a little wounded.

Eric realized his laugh had been misconstrued. He tried to think of a way to explain his laughter. He knew that explaining that he thought they were a cult at first wasn't a good idea. He figured the only way out was to tell a quick story.

"No, no. I like *The Lion King*. It holds a special place in my heart. It was the last movie my dad took me to see, before he died."

It was true. His dad had died of alcohol related heart failure when he was only a kid. One of his last memories of being with his dad was when he took him to see *The Lion King*.

An African American man stood up with tears in his eyes. He knew his story was sad but sad enough to move a stranger to tears?

"My name is Kenny. *The Lion King* is very dear to me as well," the man said in a thick accent.

Kenny continued, "I grew up in Rwanda. I was only a child when my parents and I fled the country to escape the civil war. We went from camp to camp for two years until we found ourselves in a small refugee camp in Kenya.

"One day a missionary came to the camp. He gathered all of the children together. He had brought a screen and a projector with him. He set it up and played *The Lion King* for all of us."

Kenny's voice cracked as he said, "That was the first time I could remember being happy instead of afraid."

Now Eric could feel tears in his own eyes. All he could do was nod. He wasn't alone. Across the entire room people were wiping their eyes. Some of them stood up and hugged Kenny.

Shaving

Everyone piled around the TV. Some people even sat on the floor so they could get a good view. As the movie started, Eric found himself surrounded by people who were quoting their favorite lines or laughing together.

The happiness was infectious. He found himself smiling and laughing along.

When the "I Just Can't Wait to Be King!" scene came, he found himself singing along with the entire room. When it was over everyone laughed out loud.

This party was the last thing he had expected, but it had turned out better than anything he could have hoped for.

No one was drunk or violent; no one was fighting for the attention of the girls in the room. Everyone was just getting along despite the drastic differences in backgrounds and ages.

After the movie was over, everyone sat around chatting for a while. He heard something that caught his attention.

"Buddy, did you cut yourself shaving again?"

He turned around and looked at Buddy. He hadn't noticed it earlier, but he had a new cut on his neck. It was on the opposite side this time.

"Yeah, I did it again," Buddy said.

He looked at him and asked, "Jeese Buddy, what are you shaving with, a machete?"

It took every last ounce of willpower he had to keep himself from reacting when he heard Buddy respond, "An old-fashioned straight razor."

Eric's mind kicked into high gear as he tried to sort through the implications of that. He'd just found someone who'd been in the vicinity of both crime scenes and had a straight razor.

He knew that he had to play this right. He had to be extremely careful.

After a second he came up with a game plan.

"What's that?" he asked.

"You know, one of the old-fashioned razors. The ones they used in barber shops a long time ago."

Eric continued to play stupid and just shrugged his shoulders.

"You really don't know what it is?" Buddy asked.

"No. Can you show me?" he asked.

Buddy stood up and told Eric to follow him.

They walked into the bathroom. Buddy opened the medicine cabinet and pulled out a shaving kit. He opened it up and pulled out a folding straight razor.

He realized he was holding his breath. He tried to clear his head and quickly asked, "How does it work?"

Buddy laughed and showed him how to sharpen it on a strip of leather in the kit. He then showed him what angle to use and how to get the best results.

"I'm still getting used to it. I've only had it for a couple of weeks, that's why I keep cutting myself," Buddy explained.

His mind raced. He needed to get his hands on this razor. He could get a warrant but that could take too long and could draw a lot of unwanted attention. There must be another way.

"That is so cool!" he exclaimed trying to sound as sincere as possible.

"I'll give you a hundred bucks cash for it!"

Buddy's jaw dropped and he said, "The whole kit only cost me $25 online."

Eric cocked his head and said, "Hey, supply and demand. I don't know where to get one. You have it and I want it. Deal?"

Buddy nodded quickly and started to hand the razor to him. Eric stopped him and said, "Hey, I'm paying quadruple. You can at least pack it up for me."

He was relieved when Buddy quickly packed up the kit and gently handed it to him. Now the evidence wouldn't be tainted with his prints.

"Cool. Thanks, Buddy."

The Lab

Jose, Eric, Reggie, and El Guapo were all packed in around Dr. Matsuzaka.

She slowly looked up from her workbench. Looking over her shoulder, she said in an icy voice that left no room for argument, "Only one individual at a time can look through *my* microscope. Crowding does not assist in any way. In fact, it is an annoyance, which only hinders the process."

She looked back to her bench and muttered, "Even more so considering the individual who consumed the garlic bread."

She meticulously examined the razor under her microscope. Before she even got to the end of the first side she could hear shuffling and muttering behind her. Men had no patience.

"If you want to be a distraction, please do so outside of my lab and beyond my hearing!" she spat out at them.

The room went silent.

After the inspection of the razor was done she carefully applied Luminol to the razor and changed her light filter. The razor lit up.

She picked up her voice recorder and said, "Blood is present on the razor. I am taking samples for DNA testing."

Before she even finished, excited mumbling erupted from

behind her. One look over her shoulder and the lab went silent again.

She walked over to her supply cabinet and withdrew a small slab of ballistics gel. She placed the gel on her bench and gently sliced it with the razor. She filled the incision with a fast drying plaster. After a couple of minutes, she carefully removed the plaster. She brought the plaster over to her microscope and carefully examined it. She pressed a button on the side of the microscope to capture a digital image and send it to her PC.

Taking off her gloves, she walked over to her computer. She lined up three photos and then displayed them on a large flat screen monitor.

"On the left is the mold taken from our first victim. In the middle is the mold from the second victim; they are a perfect match. On the right is the mold from this razor."

Before she could go further El Guapo grumbled, "No same."

Dr. Matsuzaka was impressed. There were only tiny differences between the murder weapon and this razor. It took a very sharp eye to pick them out.

"You are correct, Officer Hernandez," she said before she started to point out the differences in the photos on the screen.

"Are you absolutely sure?" Captain Hunter asked, with more than a little desperation in his voice.

"I could create 100 more molds, but they will never match. If they were close, I'd do two or three more. The differences are too drastic to expect a match from future molds," she said with conviction.

She watched as hope dissolved into disappointment, and four dejected men quietly shuffled out her door.

Mama Bear(s)

It was midnight when Eric got home from the forensics lab. He had to admit, no matter how badly he wanted to find the killer, he was glad it wasn't Buddy. He seemed like a good kid.

In his heart he knew that Buddy was not the killer. There was only one problem. The kid had been in the area, around the time of both killings. That meant that someone would have to keep an eye out. If Buddy did anything odd, they'd have to bring him in.

As he pulled off his shoes, he looked at the shaving kit sitting next to him. He was sure he could get reimbursed for it, but what was he going to do with it? Who actually wanted to shave with a straight razor? He was stunned there was even a market for the things. Then again, Buddy said he bought it online. He supposed that was the only way something so niche was still around.

He was so tired he couldn't even think. This case was sucking the life out of him. Every time he thought they caught a break, they ran into another wall.

He laid back and passed out cold.

He was rudely awakened by his cell phone. When he opened his eyes, daylight was streaming in from his window. He picked up his phone to see that he had slept for ten straight hours. At least it was Matt or Sally calling him, and not someone related to the case.

He slid his thumb to answer the call and in a sleepy voice said, "Hello."

He pulled the phone from his ear when it virtually exploded with, "WHO IN HEAVEN'S NAME IS SASHA COLE?!?!"

He was so shocked by the intensity of Sally's question that all he could say was, "What?"

"Suga, there is some naughty looking thang postin on your Facebook wall. She's saying all sorts of stuff. Do you need me to set her straight?" Sally said.

"No, no. She's a friend," he tried to explain.

"Oh suga, ya might want to have a lil chat with her, because she's thinking y'all is a lot more than friends," Sally replied.

"Well she's most likely right but ..."

Sally interrupted him before he could say anything else. "Suga, are you having relations with this ... girl?!?

His phone beeped to let him know he had another call. He'd never been more thankful to have a call interrupted. He prayed to God it was Jose.

"Hold on Sally. I have another call," he said as he quickly swiped his thumb to answer the other call.

A distinct Irish accent greeted him, "Paddy dear, who is

Sasha Cole?"

He now knew God was punishing him. Sally on one line, his mother on the other.

He was thankful at least that no one knew his mother called him "Paddy." Paddy was his middle name. He was given that name after his father's nickname. His dad earned it when he married his Irish mother. For a Scottish man to be called Paddy was supposed to be an insult, but his father wore it with pride.

His mother only started calling him Paddy when his dad died. He figured it brought her some comfort.

"Ma, she's a friend."

"Oh dear … you mean … what do you young people call it? Friend with benefit?"

"MA! No, it's not like that!"

"Well, are you sure she knows that? She posted some … interesting things on your Facebook."

He was mortified. He was trapped between a rock and a hard place and there was no way out.

Suddenly he thought of a plan.

"Ma, I got Sally on the other line. Hold on a sec."

He quickly pulled both calls into a three way conference.

"Can you guys hear me?"

"Yes dear," his mother replied.

"I'm here, suga," Sally kicked in.

Once they found out they were on a conference call everything changed.

"Is that you Ms. Highland?" Sally asked.

"Oh, Sally, it's so good to hear you!"

"Ms. Highland, did you know about this Sasha Cole?"

"Oh dear, no. I kept praying that Eric would meet a nice Catholic girl. I've even tried to introduce him to nice, moral, girls when he comes up to visit."

That really set Sally off because she responded, "I know what tha's like. I've tried time and again to set him up with girls with good Christian values. Did he like any of them? NO!"

He muted them and turned on the speaker.

He quickly booted up his laptop. He had to find out what Sasha had posted.

He logged onto Facebook and wondered what the big deal was. Sasha had posted: "*Had a blast the other day! Can't wait to see you again. By the way, I'm still sore!*"

What about that could have possibly have set his mama bears off?

Suddenly his eyes went wide when he figured it out. When she said she was sore they thought …

"Oh, crap!" he thought to himself.

"It's not what you guys think! We were laughing!" he yelled at his phone. He got no response. They just kept going on and on about the shameful morals of people today.

He realized he hadn't un-muted his phone.

He quickly tapped the mute button and said, "We were laughing!"

Dead silence ensued for a moment before his mother said, "Is that slang for something I don't want to know about?"

Sally piped in, "It certainly sounds like it."

"No, no! I'm sore too!" He blurted before his brain could tell him that his choice of words was awful.

"Eric Paddy Highland! I did not need to know that!" his mother scolded him.

"I can't believe you just said that to your mother! I should drive over there and wash your mouth out with soap!" a very worked up Sally responded.

"No, no, no! Our stomachs hurt the next day from laughing so hard on our date! Our stomachs were sore!" he cried out desperately.

Silence greeted him again.

Finally Sally said, "You know what I'm going to do Ms. Highland? I'm going to have these two young people over so I can sort this all out. If this … Sasha doesn't meet my standards, you better believe I'll have her running for tha hills."

"Oh Sally, you are such a dear! Thank you so much!" his mother responded before turning her attention back to him.

"Now, Eric! You won't be seeing this girl again until you introduce her to Sally. I won't have you running around down there with some harlot."

Before he could respond Sally chimed in, "Amen to that! Don't you go seein that gal till you bring her over here!"

He felt like he was back in grade school.

He tried to think of something to say but in the end could only eek out, "Yes ma'am."

More Vultures

Jose was dreading this. The last press conference had been a cakewalk. This one was going to be a living hell. The local news was already tossing around the idea of a serial killer and they didn't even know the facts.

He wondered how he was going to diffuse the crowd. He knew it was the same killer, but he couldn't tell that to the press because then they would ask what evidence he had. That was a question he could not answer without compromising the investigation.

Somehow, he had to give them just enough information to prevent a public panic, while not ruining their case in the process. How was he going to pull that off?

He stepped up to the podium and hundreds of cameras went off in a blinding flash.

He assumed his intimidating stance and forced out his power voice as he walked through only the most mundane details of the second murder. In the process, he said nothing about the first murder. He only focused on the second murder to try and subtly imply that they had nothing in common.

He finished up and asked if there were any questions. Unlike the first press conference, the room exploded in raised hands and people yelling out.

He heard one reporter ask, "Is this murder connected to

the Polynesian murder?"

"We have no concrete evidence that the two murders are related," he replied, and he wasn't wrong. There was only minimal evidence tying the crimes together. They had no fingerprints, video footage, photos, or anything else concrete. They only suspected that they were related because of the murder weapon and that evidence was flimsy at best. Until they actually found the weapon, they couldn't rely on that.

Another reporter called out, "Do the victims have anything in common?"

"Only what you already know," he replied. He wasn't about to go into details they already knew. They could piece it together.

"Do you have any suspects?" a national correspondent for CNN cried out.

"Our investigation is ongoing. At this time we do not have a suspect in custody."

He had always found that if you prefaced a non-answer with "our investigation is ongoing" it gave the impression that there was more going on, but the authorities were not going to say so yet.

"Are we dealing with a serial killer?"

"We have nothing that would lead us to believe that we are dealing with a serial killer," he replied with a hint of annoyance in his voice.

Most serial killers were exhibitionists. They left things behind on purpose or removed things from the victim. Sometimes they put the victims in a weird position. They didn't often simply kill and then leave the scene.

Personally, he was starting to think they were dealing with someone who saw people leave a hotel room and broke into it to rob the room, only to find a kid inside. It was a weak theory, but it was all he had.

All the other questions pouring in were just rehashes of questions he'd already answered or covered in his opening statements.

"We'd like to ask the public to be alert and let us know if they see anything that seems out of place. Thank you!"

He stepped down and saw a very haggard looking Reggie nodding his approval.

If they didn't catch a break soon he wasn't sure Reggie was going to survive.

Cars and Questions

Sasha had been psyched when Eric finally got around to asking her out on another date. She'd been even happier to find out that he wanted to introduce her to his friends. That had to be a good sign.

Before the date, she had mentally made a list of some seemingly simple questions to ask Eric. The questions would tell her a lot. She'd found that some simple questions could give amazing insight into a person. One of her first questions was going to be whether she should get braces. There was no way she was going to get them. That wasn't the point of the question. She had one slightly crooked tooth on the top of her mouth. She thought it added to her personality and gave her a "real" look. She couldn't stand people who felt the need to look like Barbie.

Her simple question would let her know if Eric was overly superficial or not. She'd found that the "braces" question had worked very well over the years. She had cut off more than one guy, after he had answered it wrong. Seriously, who wanted to date a guy who didn't want you, but instead wanted to turn you into something you were not?

The first and foremost test was the car. She had purposefully asked Eric to pick her up so she could see his car. If he showed up in an unmarked police cruiser, she was going to be disappointed. That wouldn't tell her anything. If he showed up in a mod car, she might just walk back into the small rundown home she rented.

God, did she ever hate mod cars. People with street racers typically raced once in a blue moon; most of the time they just made noise, drove like jerks, and expected other people to stare at their "cool" car. Most of them were too stupid to realize that 99% of the people were staring, not out of jealousy, but to see what kind of a douche bag was behind the wheel.

She smiled when Eric pulled up driving a simple, stock VW. That was perfect. He didn't feel the need to impress her with his car. That was always a good thing. It normally meant he'd focus his energies on more important areas.

As she walked down to his car, she noticed the concerned look on his face.

"This is a rough neighborhood," he said as she walked up and hugged him.

She could tell by the way he said it that it was not a dig on her, it was statement motivated by concern. That was cute.

She pulled away, looked up at him and said with a fake British accent, "Hey don't knock it, it's cheap!"

She was amazed to see, not a look of confusion, but of recognition spread across his face.

"Lock Stock," he said, nodding.

She had only met two other people who had even seen the Guy Ritchie film. She'd never met anyone who could quote it. She mentally added another big check to the plus column in her head.

They chitchatted as they drove down the road. After a few minutes she felt it was time to start pulling out the important questions.

"Do you think I should get braces?" she asked.

He looked at her out of the corner of his eye and said, "What? Why would you do that?"

She put on a big smile and said, "Look, I have a crooked tooth."

He smiled and said, "So what? I kinda like it. It's cute."

Sasha tried to hold in her excitement. That was as close to a perfect answer as you could expect out of a guy. Another girl would have answered it better, but guys weren't as skilled when it came to compliments.

She decided to try to spin the tables on him and see how he reacted.

"So, babe, how long have you had this car?"

He fell right into her trap.

"Babe? I don't think anyone has ever called me babe before. That seems like a better fit for you," he replied.

She grinned and bit her bottom lip before saying, "So you think I'm a babe?"

She knew she had hit her mark when he started to turn bright red, which was a very good sign. Any guy who didn't blush every now and then couldn't be trusted. They typically were self centered or so messed up you'd be better off jumping out of a moving car, than spending any more time with them.

Sasha realized that part of her was concerned. She had no checks in her negative column yet. She always wanted at least a check or two before she got too attached. She didn't want to get blindsided by something big once it would hurt to break it off.

"So, why did it take you so long to ask me out again?" she asked.

She realized it hadn't been long at all, but she wanted to see what he would say. If he argued that could show a stubborn streak or even a slight temper. If he came up with an excuse, that could reveal some other negative.

"I've been really busy with work," he explained.

She nodded and put a check in the negative column, but it was a very small one. All it meant was he had responsibilities that she was going to take second place to from time to time. That was okay. At least he was employed, and actually worked hard. That was better than a lot of guys she'd met.

She felt frustration growing inside of her. He wasn't the cause. She was frustrated with herself. There were just way too many checks in the "plus" column. She was falling for him, and couldn't stop, or even slow it down. Less than two dates was way too fast. Maybe she should just let go and let it happen? She really wanted to, but the idea scared her.

Meet the Millers

Eric hoped to God that Sasha didn't try to hold his hand as he got out of the car in front of Matt and Sally's house. His hands were drenched with sweat. He couldn't remember the last time he'd been this nervous.

Sasha walked up to him, put her arm through his, and smiled. After a moment she said, "Are we going in, or are they going to bring the food out and lay it on your car?"

He gave a nervous laugh and together they started for the door. He was worried because he knew Sasha had no idea what she was getting herself into.

He pushed the doorbell and waited. He realized Sally was playing games. She was always at the window waiting when she expected company. He couldn't remember the last time he'd had a chance to knock on the door before Sally opened it.

When the door opened, it took all of his willpower not to shove Sasha through the door and run for his life.

Sally greeted them with a big smile. She leaned in and hugged him, but only shook Sasha's hand. That was a very bad sign. Sally hugged everyone and everything. A guy could have just crawled out of a cesspool and Sally would run right up and hug him without thinking twice.

When he walked into the living room, things were even worse; Sally had set up lemonade and some cheese and crackers. Sally did not host people in the living room. When you went over to Matt and Sally's, you were brought right into the kitchen.

This wasn't going to be a dinner. It was going to be an interrogation.

Everyone sat down, and Matt lumbered in from the kitchen. He greeted Sasha and gave her a hug. The look that appeared on Sally's face could have melted the paint off of the walls. He did everything he could to not make eye contact.

"So Sasha, where are you from?" Sally asked with a big fake smile on her face.

"I grew up in Boise."

"Oh, Eric is from the Northeast too," Sally replied.

He manage to keep his face straight. Sasha also did well and kept her smile on. Matt, however ...

"Boise isn't in the Northeast!" he boomed with a thunderous laugh.

Matt was book smart. He had a good knowledge of a number of subjects, and had picked up a lot of facts in his time. Learning to think before he spoke was not one of them.

"Rhode Island is so in the Northeast!" Sally spat back.

Eric assumed that Matt would have caught on to the fact that he needed to shut his trap. He was wrong.

"Woman, Bosie is in Idaho!" Matt bellowed as he started to laugh harder.

He could swear he could see red lights start to glow in Sally's eyes, but then she made it even worse.

"Ok so it's in the Midwest! I was only off by a few states"

Matt had to sit down he was laughing so hard. He finally composed himself and said, "Idaho is in the Northwest next to Washington and Oregon."

Sally finally snapped. He had never seen her snap before. He was just glad it wasn't on Sasha.

"You know what, you big lug?!? You can kiss my grits!" she yelled at Matt.

He cringed as a small laugh escaped from Sasha.

Sally turned on her and said, "What's so funny? I may not be book smart like y'all, but it doesn't mean I'm stupid!"

Eric just looked down at his lap. He still didn't know a lot about Sasha, but he knew two things for sure: she was feisty and she wasn't afraid to stand her ground.

"Your choice of insults is what's funny. Seriously who says "kiss my grits?" That has to be the biggest southern cliché there is."

At first he thought Sally was going to fly across the room, grab Sasha by the neck, and throw her out, but then she started laughing. It occurred to him that she didn't take that as an attack. Sally was a proud southerner.

"Only true southerners say that," Sally said with a smile.

He slowly let out the breath he'd been holding. He hoped no one had noticed that he was sweating bullets.

"So, how did you two meet?" Sally asked.

"When I met you guys for the first time," Sasha replied.

He saw that Matt and Sally both looked confused. He could tell their minds were racing. They were trying to figure out when they had met her.

Before they could make the connection, Sasha pulled a framed photo out of her messenger bag.

"It took me a while to find this. A lot of people come through every day. I didn't have the photo number so I had to go through all the ones from that day to find it," Sasha said as she passed the framed photo to Sally.

Sally looked confused. Matt sat next to her and looked at the photo.

Suddenly Matt cried out, "Holy shit, you're Mickey Mouse!"

"Language!" Sally cried out as she elbowed Matt hard in

the ribs, but then all of what he had said registered.

"OH GOOD HEAVENS! You're Mickey Mouse!" she cried out.

Sally looked back down at the photo and a tear came to her eye. "This is such a wonderful gift! It's the first time we met!" she said.

She jumped up, ran across the room and wrapped Sasha in a big bear hug.

He figured his mother would be getting a stellar report soon.

Late to the Party

Jose sat back in the wicker chair on his porch. It was a nice evening and he needed to unwind. He planned to sit there and suck down mojitos till the sun went down.

He was bone tired. He had really pushed himself at the gym earlier, but that wasn't the only reason for his fatigue. This case was mentally draining. It was worse than any other case he'd ever been on.

"Who is Sasha Cole?" his girlfriend, Jenica, asked as she joined him outside.

The tone in her voice made him panic at first. He didn't know anyone by that name, so he should be safe, but he still didn't like the tone.

If Jenica was one thing, she was jealous. He didn't mind too much. They'd been together for two years. Those had been two fun years.

Jenica was a feisty Cuban. Not just feisty, but wild. He often swore she had two emotional modes: overdrive and tidal wave. She either displayed a lot of emotion, or an overwhelming amount of emotion, and that's why he loved her. He never had to guess where he stood with Jenica. She was more than willing to let him know.

She sat down on his lap and put her arms around his neck. "It seems like your buddy is tapping some lil' blonde thing," she said bluntly.

"Who, Eric? No way, the only girls he meets are in his dreams. That guy has about as much game as a dead monkey."

"I know what I saw and I saw it on his Facebook. Before you go questioning me why don't you take five seconds out of your pressing business out here to look for yourself," she said as she shook her head.

He gave her a naughty grin and leaned toward her.

"Oh no you don't! You better answer my question before even thinking about getting any of this," she said as she stood up and glared at him.

He sat back and pulled out his iPhone. He pulled up Facebook and jumped over to Eric's page. He didn't check it often because the man almost never updated it. Right there on the wall was an interesting post from a Sasha Cole.

He grinned and said, "Well look at that! Our little buddy found a friend. Oh man, am I ever going to bust his chops over this."

He dialed Eric's number. It rang a few times and when Eric picked up, he could tell he was on the Bluetooth receiver, in the man's car. He could hear the hum of the engine in the background.

He didn't even wait, he just jumped right in. "Yo, Eric. You smashing some girl named Sasha?" he asked as a smile spread across his face.

The smile fell right off his face when a female voice responded, "Excuse me? We are not sleeping together. Who told you that?"

He was so shocked he couldn't respond. Thankfully, Eric mentioned the post she had left on his wall.

"Who would think that? What kind of lewd person would assume such a thing?" Jose heard the female voice respond.

That really made him smile as he looked up at Jenica.

"What are you smiling at?" Jenica asked when she saw him looking at her.

He muted his phone and said, "Looks like our little buddy has himself a feisty one, but they aren't sleeping together. You wanna meet her?"

That made Jenica smile. "You know it," she said.

He unmuted his phone and said, "Hey, why don't you swing by so we can meet your girl. She sounds feisty. Did you finally take my advice and find yourself a good Latina? You know, like the ones you're always staring at when we're hanging out."

He quickly muted the phone again as he and Jenica started to laugh. He made sure to turn on the speaker before anyone had time to respond.

"You have a thing for Hispanic girls? Maybe you couldn't tell by the blonde hair, light eyes, and pale skin, but I'm not exactly a Latina."

That response had him laughing so hard he almost fell out of his chair.

"Jose, we are heading over. Not so you can meet Sasha. So I can kick your ass," Eric said, trying to sound serious.

This time, he did fall out of his chair.

Tension

The next morning, Jose, Eric, Reggie, Dr. Matsuzaka, Victor, and Fidel were once again seated in the small conference room they used for case meetings. The last time they had met, things had been very serious. This time, the tension was so high it made the hair on the back of Jose's neck stand up.

"So what do we know?" asked Reggie in a weary voice.

Jose assumed his normal role and said, "We know the following:

"It appears the same murder weapon was used to commit both murders.

"In both cases, the security system tells us that a family member opened the door.

"In both cases, the parents left their child behind in a locked room.

"In both cases, the murderer used the stairs to avoid security cameras.

"Both murders were shockingly clean. We don't even have partial fingerprints or traces of the murderer's clothes.

"Both victims were males between 10 and 12 years old.

"There were no items unaccounted for in either case."

After a moment of silence, Reggie asked, "Any theories?"

When no one responded, Jose said, "I think they could be botched robberies. There have been some robberies in which it appears a cast member has been using room keys or RFID readers assigned to the guests to enter their rooms. We could be dealing with someone who was monitoring the rooms and saw two adults leave and didn't expect to find a child inside."

Victor chimed in, "It's just a theory, though. Prior to these two, all of the unauthorized entries were at the Animal Kingdom Lodge."

Reggie looked up and said, "It's at least something. Maybe the killer felt he had to move on to other resorts to avoid detection? Is there anything that could tip us off as to where he could strike next?"

"The Grand Floridian," Eric said.

Everyone in the room looked at Eric, but no one said anything, and Eric didn't explain.

Finally Victor asked, "Why do you think the Grand Floridian is next?"

Eric looked up and said, "It's the final hotel on the Monorail. If they are starting to display a pattern based on location, that is going to be the next place they hit."

Jose scratched his head. The whole premise was crap. It

was founded on large leaps of logic and assumptions, but they didn't have anything else.

"We'll set up hidden, wireless cameras on all floors and get a remote command center established there," Victor said.

"Maybe we get lucky," Fidel said as he tried to sound encouraging.

It didn't work. No one was saying so, but this was a long shot and they all knew it.

Long shots were all they had left.

One in a Million

Eric was bored out of his mind. He sat in the Grand Floridian's Wedding Pavilion, which had been temporarily turned into their war room. Nothing had happened. He felt like they were just wasting time.

He'd already blasted through all of his ideas to distract himself. He'd started by walking around the resort. The entire time he'd had a persistent feeling he'd seen the hotel before. The red roof, white paint, and architecture all nagged at him. He assumed Disney had stolen the look from somewhere and recreated it so well that it was giving him déjà vu.

It was a pleasant place to walk. The resort had a lot of nice features, but it also felt like it had a stick up its butt. He'd walked by some fancy sounding restaurant and received a look that told him he wouldn't even be allowed to look inside dressed the way he was. He decided that instead of its real name, he was going to call that place Berkley and Jensen, after the generic BJ's wholesale brand.

That's how bored he was. He was renaming things. He renamed another restaurant Citrus Suckers after he saw the prices. Charging that much for Mediterranean food should be a crime, considering he could get it outside of Disney for less than half the price.

The resort was so big it had two other sit down restaurants. One he'd renamed Ahchooiees and another he just referred to as the place with the characters.

Then there was the pool. He didn't know if you could classify it as a pool when it was bigger than some of the lakes in Florida.

The main lobby was impressive. It was a huge open space with chandeliers and Victorian accents. After a moment, he decided that even though it was impressive, he liked the concourse in the Contemporary better.

After he walked around for a while he started texting people. He started with Buddy. He figured if anyone would know why this placed looked so familiar, it would be him.

He was right. Buddy informed him that the Grand Floridian was based on a number of Victorian Era hotels, including the Mt. Washington Resort in Bretton Woods, New Hampshire.

As soon as he read that, he kicked himself. He'd been by the Mt. Washington on a day trip he and his buddies had taken in college. He had to admit the Mt. Washington was one impressive building. Not only was it original to the era, but its surroundings were absolutely striking. There was no way Disney could match that without constructing 5000' mountains all around the resort. Part of him was surprised Disney didn't attempt that.

After he was done texting Buddy, he texted Sasha. That only left him bummed that he had to work. She had the day off.

"You should transfer to restaurant in GF. Looks like easier

gig."

She responded, "*No way. Don't wanna be FC.*"

"*FC?*"

"*Face character. No head. Like Marry Pops, the Princesses, and Alice. They get paid more.*"

"*Then why not?*"

"*Can't stick tongue out, mutter, or make faces at people -I go nuts W-O that.*"

He figured she was right. The extra dollar or so wouldn't be worth losing the ability to make faces at people without them knowing.

They exchanged a few more texts and then she made things 1000 times worse. She sent him a text that said "*wish you were here*" and a photo came with it of her in her in a bra with a sad face.

After seeing that, he strongly thought about banging his head against the wall till he passed out. He figured it was the only thing that could keep him here.

Instead, he passively watched the video feeds in front of him. They had half of them wired here and the other half at the security office. Victor and Fidel were at the office with a couple of the resort's security team. He and Jose were here at the staging area. The idea was they'd be able to hit any area fast since they were spread out.

"Are you going to do a walk-through on the second victim?" Jose asked him.

He just shook his head and explained, "I didn't see a point. The victims' days were almost identical. The only real differences are where they were killed and the order they visited the attractions."

He truly felt awful that his walk-through hadn't helped him find any clues. All it did was motivate him to find the killer. At this point he was beyond motivated. When he closed his eyes at night, he saw two sets of lifeless eyes staring back at him. It gave him nightmares. He'd had one where the two bodies were lying next to each other. Their lips had been silently moving. He couldn't physically hear their voices but instead heard them in his head. Their words were muttered and ran together. He couldn't make out what they were trying to say.

He shook his head in an attempt to clear that visual from his memory.

"When are you seeing Sasha again?" Jose asked, an attempt to pass the time.

He just muttered, "As soon as possible."

That got a laugh out of Jose who replied, "I can understand that."

"How are you and Jenica doing?"

Jose looked to see if anyone was around before whispering, "Do you really want to know?"

He was suddenly very concerned. He didn't know how to take that question.

Jose reached into his suit jacket and pulled out a distinctive robin's egg colored box. He opened it up to display a sparkling engagement ring.

His eyes nearly bulged out of his head. He quickly responded, "Jose, I like you and all, and I know that's legal in most states now, but I like girls."

Jose leaned back and gave him a dirty look before saying, "You can be a real ass sometimes."

"Isn't that why you love me? I don't think you got the right size though. It's looks too small for my finger."

They both burst out laughing.

After they composed themselves Eric said, "It's about time. I can't imagine anyone else putting up with you."

"Me?" Jose said wounded, "What about her?"

He cracked a smile and said, "Oh spare me. She looks like J-Lo and her body is just as tight."

Jose gave him a sideways glance and asked, "You been checking out my woman?"

At that they both broke out laughing again.

"But, in all seriousness, I'm happy for you. Unless she says no, then I'll be really happy for you," he said and busted out laughing again.

Jose looked at him, put on a serious face and said, "You know what that means? I'm going to need a best man."

Eric stopped laughing and said, "Wouldn't miss it for the world," and they bumped fists.

Jose leaned back in his chair and said, "I'll watch for a while. Why don't you go get us some coffee?"

"Sir! Yes, Sergeant Ortega, sir!" he belted out.

"Oh God, don't start that crap, rookie."

Before he could get up, their radio went off, "Something we got!" came El Guapo's excited voice.

Eric bolted forward in his seat.

Jose was so startled he tipped over backward and spilled onto the floor.

He grabbed the radio and called back, "What is it?"

"We are sending the feeds now," came Victor's voice this time.

A video feed popped up on his screen. It was dated from

this morning.

"Watch closely," Victor said.

The feed started. He and Jose watched as a cleaning lady opened a room door and struggled to push her cleaning cart through. Another cast member came up and held the door open for her. After she had entered the room the second cast member quickly stuck something in the latch.

"You catch that?" El Guapo asked.

Unless they had been tipped off, he never would have noticed the subtle movement.

"Yes, he stuck something in the latch," he said.

"Exactly," came Victor's voice, "Now watch this."

The feed changed to only a couple of minutes ago. They watched as a young couple left the room.

"They are our guests. They have an ADR at the Hoop Dee Doo, over in Fort Wilderness," explained Victor before continuing, "Guess who shows up a couple of minutes later?"

They watched as the cast member from earlier in the day appeared. He looked around and inserted something into the latch. The door swung open. He looked closely at the video feed and gasped.

"Jose, look! He has gloves on."

Jose grabbed the radio and called out, "Everyone, converge on that room now! Office team, approach from the far side. We'll approach from the near side."

Together they bolted out of the wedding pavilion and across the resort.

They'd entered the building where the room was located and hit the stairs. In less than a minute, they made the third floor. They saw Victor and El Guapo on the far side of the long hallway. They nodded to them and all started forward at the same time.

They approached the door as quietly as they could and stopped out front. Eric put his shoulder against the doorjamb and pulled out his gun. El Guapo put this shoulder against the opposite jamb and did the same. Jose stood in the middle, drew his gun and nodded to the two of them and then to Victor. Victor swiped his security badge in front of a sensor and the latch buzzed.

Jose burst through the door in the blink of an eye. Eric followed right on his heels, with Fidel close behind.

"Freeze! OCSD!" Jose yelled.

In the middle of the room stood a startled cast member holding a laptop. In a matter of seconds Jose had him face down on the floor and cuffed.

Carefully they searched him. Eric reached into his pocket; what he felt made his eyes go wide.

Jose noticed and asked, "What is it?"

He slowly pulled a folding box cutter out of the man's pocket. The blade on the box cutter looked almost identical to a straight razor.

Elation

Eric and Jose looked at the man through a one-way window. He looked ordinary, but most of the murderers they'd busted over the years did. He still had his cast member uniform on too; name tag and all.

"That's why we found the victims in front of the door," Jose said.

He nodded and said, "Yeah, after seeing smiling cast members all day long, they wouldn't have thought twice about approaching one."

He thought back to his walk-through, and it fit. Every cast member he'd seen had been smiling and happy. It would have drawn a kid like a moth to a flame.

Everything was falling into place. The crime scene was cleared and they had caught the guy red-handed. Dr. Matsuzaka was analyzing the murder weapon now, but when she first saw it, she said it could have inflicted the wounds she saw on the victims.

Reggie walked into the room. He seemed like he was walking on air, "Damn good job, you two! Now get in there and make that son of a bitch sing! I'll call the DA and get a warrant for his house."

Jose looked at Reggie and nodded.

Eric felt like he was floating as he followed Jose into the

interrogation room. He felt even better when he saw the suspect. He wasn't as good as Jose when it came to judging body language, but he could tell this man felt cornered.

They hadn't said a word before the suspect said, "I admit it. I've been breaking into rooms and stealing things for months."

Jose glared at the man. His gaze was so intense that it almost made him flinch.

"What about the kids?" Jose growled.

The suspect put on a confused look and looked between Eric and Jose.

"How do you know about that?" the suspect said as he started to cry.

Jose smiled. They had him.

"It's my thing. I look, but never touch. I got all the photos from chat rooms. I swear I didn't take any of them!" the suspect choked out between sobs.

Eric looked at Jose and saw him staring back. He knew they were both thinking the same thing. This guy was admitting to other crimes, in an attempt to deflect their attention from the murders.

Jose laid two photos in front of the suspect. "What about these children?" he asked.

The suspect's eyes went wide when he saw the victims. He shook his head and said "no" over and over again.

"No, you didn't do it, or no, you can't believe we found out?" he asked.

The suspect was shaking now. He sat back and looked at Jose. They knew what they had to do now. Once you rattled a suspect and they didn't admit to the crime, you had to change tactics.

By the time they had changed tactics twice, the suspect had a hard time remembering his name. He knew it was only a matter of time before the guy cracked.

A few minutes later, the door to the interrogation room opened. Reggie walked in, followed by two other detectives.

"What's going on? This is our case, Captain," Jose protested.

"Detectives Winterberry and Smith will be taking over the interrogation. Come with me," Reggie said softly.

The tone of the Captain's voice bothered him. Something was definitely up.

Eric and Jose stood up and followed Reggie to his office. Reggie sat down at his desk and pulled open a drawer. He pulled a bottle of Old Crow whiskey and a glass out of the drawer. He filled the glass with nearly eight ounces of whiskey and then drank it down in four huge gulps.

"Captain?" Eric asked in shock.

Reggie didn't even look up he just stared at his glass for a moment before saying in a flat, apathetic voice, "The Wilderness Lodge."

Eric looked at Jose in time to see the blood drain from his face.

The Lodge

Eric and Jose arrived at the Wilderness Lodge thirty minutes after being dispatched by Captain Hunter. They stepped out of their cars and didn't say a word as they headed toward the main entrance.

A familiar face greeted them. "Hi Er ..." Buddy started to say until Jose shifted his imposing glare in Buddy's direction, stopping the nervous cast member dead in his tracks.

"Buddy, this is Sergeant Jose Ortega," he said.

Jose reached his hand out toward Buddy and said, "Nice to meet you."

Buddy was so nervous he couldn't speak. He just reached out and shook Jose's hand.

They followed Buddy into the main lobby. Despite everything he had already seen in Disney World, he was once again surprised.

The main lobby was a large open space. All around were dark wood accents, exposed beams and stone work. It looked like someone had picked up a national park lodge in the Northwest and dropped it in Florida. The place had an overwhelming feeling of serenity, which was enhanced by a log fire crackling in a massive stone hearth. The only thing in the room that seemed slightly out of place was a large totem pole in one of the corners. That was something he would have expected to see outdoors, not in a lobby.

They continued to follow Buddy across the lobby and something else grabbed his attention. There was what appeared to be a natural spring in the lobby. The water bubbled up out of the floor, ran under a small bridge and then out the wall.

They passed through a glass door next to the spot where the spring flowed out of the building. Outside, they followed the stream of water down toward the lake. The spring flowed through a well-themed area and ended when it flowed off a stone ledge and crashed into the swimming pool.

Eric was so distracted by it that he jumped when he heard a hiss in front of them. Between them and the lake was a geyser, just starting to erupt.

He just shook his head and kept walking. He decided that some day he was going to check out all the Disney resorts. He didn't doubt you could spend a day or two just wandering through all of the ridiculously detailed resorts.

They arrived at their destination. What greeted them made his stomach twist in a knot. Victor was next to the door like he had been at the other crime scenes. This time, however, he was sitting on the floor with his back against the wall. His head was leaning on the wall and his eyes were closed. He looked utterly defeated.

"What's the deal, Victor?" Jose asked as they approached.

Victor didn't move, he didn't even open his eyes; he just sat there and said, "We've got another one inside. This one is worse than the others."

Eric and Jose pressed into the room. It was never easy to see a dead child, but this hit him hard. It paralyzed him. The kid was wearing Matt's monorail hat. On one of the beds was a monorail play set. The whole scene made it feel like someone had punched him in the stomach.

The body lay in the same place as the others, only a few feet from the door. The wound appeared to be exactly the same as the other victims.

Although it was disturbing, he couldn't see why this scene was worse than the others they'd processed. He looked at Jose and saw tears streaking down his cheeks. The sight stunned him. He'd never seen Jose cry. In five years of working horrific crime scenes, nothing had ever made Jose cry.

He looked back at the body. After a moment he noticed a detail that was so overwhelming he felt his knees start to give out. Tears filled his eyes and ran down his face. He found it hard to breathe.

The victim was wearing a t-shirt with purple lettering that said "Give Kids the World."

This victim was a terminally ill child.

Rage

Jose hung on the long flat section of the cliffhanger. He'd blasted through the initial sections of the obstacle. Now before him was his nemesis. Below, the usual crowd had gathered to cheer him on. Even Eric was here today, and Jose knew why.

Sometimes when all you felt was anger, the only thing that could get rid of it was hardcore exercise. You had to push yourself till you dropped. If you didn't, the anger would stubbornly hold on to your soul. You had to shed it. If you allowed it to stay, it would rear its ugly head and you'd find yourself lashing out at friends and family. Some people tried to drown it with alcohol, but that was only a temporary solution.

Jose felt anger build inside of him like an out-of-control fire. He was beyond angry. He didn't want to bring the murderer to justice anymore; he wanted to hunt the bastard down and beat on him until no one would recognize the remains as a body.

With a roar, Jose launched himself toward the small lip. He reached it like he had in his last attempt, when his fingers and forearms couldn't hold and he had crashed to the mats below. Last time he had been annoyed. This time he was infuriated. His fingers latched onto the lip like a vice.

When he didn't fall, a roar erupted from behind him. They'd never seen anyone make it this far, except on TV.

Jose knew he wasn't done. There was still the final transition. This one was longer, and had a bigger drop, but the lip was longer, so he didn't have to be quite as accurate when he jumped.

His forearms were starting to burn. He knew he didn't have much time. In one quick motion, he launched himself at the next lip. Focusing everything he had, channeling all of his anger and rage at that tiny ledge, he snarled as he grabbed at it. The force pulling him down was tremendous, but somehow his fingers held.

This time, there was only silence; he could almost hear everyone holding their breath. They were waiting to see if he could finish.

He wasted no time. He shuffled down the final lip and planted his feet on the platform.

He flexed his arms in his best bodybuilder pose and let out an enormous roar.

Everyone else exploded into pandemonium.

Eric hugged him after he hopped down from the platform. All the other spectators took turns high-fiving or chest bumping him.

Within minutes, five guys had lined up to take a shot at the brutal obstacle. They had renewed motivation. They had seen firsthand that it was possible. Jose took some solace in the fact that he had given them hope. Now he just wished someone would return the favor.

His anger was gone. Now there was only an empty pit where it had been. He suddenly felt very tired. Every part of his body felt like it weighed too much for him to bear.

He looked up to see Eric, who looked like he felt the same way.

Their souls were crushed.

Distracted

Eric pushed the food around on his plate. He really wasn't hungry, and he was in a terrible mood. He knew he should snap out of it. He was being awful company.

He looked across the table to see Sasha glaring at him. Then she smiled and said, "At least I'm not the one paying."

That made him feel even worse. He had planned this date himself. They were supposed to be having a relaxing dinner at his favorite restaurant. He couldn't afford to eat at Texas de Brazil on a regular basis. It was one of those places that hurt when you got the bill, but you never complained because it was worth every dollar.

This was the place he went on special occasions. He brought his friends here when he got promoted to Detective. He'd brought Jose and Jenica here for their anniversary. He brought his mother and sister here when they came to visit. Now he'd brought Sasha here and he was ruining it.

"I know it's drastically different, but I leave work at work. I'm not thinking about the kid who blew chunks all over me the other day," Sasha said as she tried to cheer him up. All he could manage was a smirk so she tried again.

"It was gross too. That kid had been eating popcorn and Mickey Mouse bars."

He glanced down at his plate, then looked up and gave her a grimace.

"Don't even think about giving me a dirty look! You weren't eating anyway."

He wiped the look off his face and said, "Maybe all that talk about popcorn and ice cream made me hungry."

She looked back at him and said, "If that made you hungry, you can thank me, but then never call me again because that's just nasty!"

He couldn't help himself. He started laughing and shaking his head.

"That's better! Since I made you smile does that mean I get a second drink and the death by chocolate cake? You know the one I mean. The chocolate cake with chocolate ice cream covered with hot fudge and shaved milk chocolate!"

He gave her a sideways glance and said, "How can I argue with that? You can also have as many drinks as you want, as long as they are not Irish Car Bombs."

She didn't miss a beat and came right back with, "Oh, no, not in a place like this. Those make me burp. I think they'd kick you out of a place like this for burping."

By the time the waiter came back to check on the meal, he had eaten most of it. Somehow Sasha had found a way to make him forget the killings for a little while.

"Could we order some drinks?" he asked.

The waiter perked right up and said "Certainly!"

He looked at Sasha and said, "Ladies first."

He watched as she jokingly looked around and then pointed to herself with a questioning look on her face.

He started laughing and nodded.

"I'll have a Long Island Iced Tea, please," she said.

He couldn't keep the shock off his face.

She caught him and said, "What? You're driving, Romeo."

He ordered a mint julep.

"Mint julep? What are you 90? I don't even think the people at the Kentucky Derby like drinking those. They just have to because they're at the Kentucky Derby."

He gave her an injured look and said, "Hey, I like mint juleps. Plus, they are making a comeback!"

She laughed and said, "Yeah, here in Florida. You know what they call Florida? It's the land of the newlyweds and nearly-deads. I assure you, the newlyweds are not drinking mint juleps."

They sipped their drinks for a while. Despite his best

efforts, he started to slip back into his bad mood. Sasha noticed immediately, and wasn't about to let him get away with it.

"Why don't you tell me about it?" she said.

He shook his head and said, "I don't think that will help."

She just stared at him and said, "It's not for your benefit. I'll be better able to put up with you if I know what's going on."

Once again she had managed to back him into a corner.

He didn't go into detail about the murders. She already knew the basics from the news. Instead, he tried to explain why it bothered him, exactly why he was so frustrated. He finished by telling her about the nightmares he'd been having.

She just looked at him, shook her head, and said, "I can't imagine walking into a room and having the first thing you see be a dead body. Never mind it being a kid. I don't know how the parents are dealing with it. If it was my kid, I think I'd end it all. I don't know if I could deal with that."

He leaned forward and said, "That's what's even worse. The parents are putting all their hope in us and I feel like we are totally failing them. If we can't catch the guy they will never be able to start healing."

Sasha picked up her drink and downed it. She then looked him with a pained look and squeaked out, "Are you sure you don't want … or need one of these?"

He smiled and said, "No. Getting tipsy would just make things worse."

She nodded and said, "Then, pay the bill. We're headed back to my place. I know something that will cheer you up."

He didn't mean to, but his eyes shot open at that remark.

She looked at him and shook her head, "Not that, you pig. You think hanging out with the human equivalent of Eeyore puts me in the mood? In fact, I think if you Google ways to turn a girl off, acting like Eeyore would be near the top."

Everything Has a Story

They arrived at Sasha's house less than an hour later. Eric followed her to the front door and waited as she opened it. He noticed that after she unlocked the deadbolt and doorknob, she pulled up on the door and pushed.

"It's a trick door. The doorjamb is warped. The landlord is too cheap to fix it," she explained with a smile.

He thought the peeling exterior was banged up. Inside was very clean, but old and worn. The place looked like it was falling apart. It looked like someone had painted the crumbling walls when they should have torn them down and put up new drywall. He noticed that the floor was cheap vinyl tiles and very slick. If he wasn't careful his leather bottomed shoes would slide right out from under him.

The air smelled like a flower mixed with something earthy. He couldn't place it.

"Is that a candle or air freshener?"

She looked over her shoulder and said, "Yeah, sorry. I don't think the last renters were very clean. I've cleaned again and again, but sometimes it still smells funky so I use a lot of Febreze."

As they walked in, he felt a little out of sorts. It took him a moment to notice that the floor was slightly tilted.

She noticed he seemed off kilter and said, "Ah, you noticed the fun house effect! I've given up hoping that gets fixed. It can come in handy. Drinking only makes the effect worse, so when my friends come over, I know to cut them off if they stagger when crossing the room."

He guessed that was an outstanding example of making lemonade from life's lemons.

He looked around the small living room. Sasha didn't have much, but it looked like she made the most of what she did have. He could see that she had put some 2x4s under the couch where a leg had broken off. Instead of just leaving it like that, she had painted it to blend in. She had window treatments on the windows, but they didn't match directly. They were all from different Disney movies.

"It's a fun collection of window treatments," he said as he smiled at her.

She shrugged her shoulders and admitted, "I've never seen most of them. I guess they were mostly flops because they ended up giving them away. I get my stuff where I can. I'm not afraid to pick up free or secondhand stuff. I guess I'm one of the rare people who doesn't use a credit card and lives within their means."

"One thing I have developed from living below the poverty line is anathema for people who think they are better or smarter than others, just because they have more. I've met a lot of stupid people who fell ass backward into great jobs or huge amounts of money, while some really smart people have gotten one bad break after another and ended up on the street," she said as she looked around at her collection of odds and ends.

"I like your stuff. It has character and I bet everything you have in here has a story behind it," he said as he looked her in the eye.

She perked up and said, "You bet! She pointed over to her small tube TV and said, "That was my grammy's. She didn't have much. She sold most of her stuff to pay for medical bills, but she didn't sell that. We used to sit in front of it and watch Carol Burnett together. She loved Carol Burnett."

He saw her eyes moisten and she said, "Other than a few photos, that's all I have from her."

Sasha walked over to a small side table against the wall and picked up a framed photo. She walked over and showed it to him. It was a photo of an elderly lady and a young girl with a bowl cut in front of Cinderella's castle.

"Is that your grammy?" he asked.

Sasha nodded and said, "That was just before she died. I'd never been happier. Not even when my parents were alive."

He hugged her close and kissed her on the forehead, "I hope I can make you that happy someday. No, not hope. I'm going to make you that happy."

She didn't say anything; she just hugged him back.

Road Rage

Sasha walked over to her small TV and opened up the cabinet underneath it. She smiled at Eric and said, "Check this out."

She proudly displayed her Nintendo Wii to him.

"It was a cast member giveaway. It came with a game called Epic Mickey. I like to say I won it because I'm the real life "Epic Mickey," she said as she gave him her best grin.

He may have been acting like Eeyore earlier, but he more than made up for it with his promise to make her happy. It wasn't often a guy said the right thing but when they did, you had to give them a break. If you didn't, they'd probably never get a break, because most of the time they said the dumbest things or tried to fix something you didn't want fixed.

"My friends chipped in and got me these bad boys!" she pulled out two white, plastic steering wheels with Wii remotes in them.

She handed one to him and said, "I hope you're ready to get your butt kicked by a girl!"

He gave her a cocky smile and said, "We'll see about that."

She just shook her head. Out of all the responses he could have made, he had to say something dumb like that. He could have said something fun like "I might enjoy that," but he didn't. Now she wasn't going to go easy on him. She had mad Mario Kart skills and he was going to find that out the hard way.

After three races she was in first place and he was halfway down the pack. Three times in a row he had been in first within sight of the finish line. Three times she had saved a weapon for the last second and nailed him with it, making him crash and fall way back.

He tried to pull that trick on her for the fourth race. She saw it coming, slowed down and flicked her wrist. Her character slammed into his, which caused him to run into a giant penguin. He finished last that round.

"This seems like something Buddy would play," he said as they started the next round.

"Who's Buddy?" she asked.

"He's a friend of mine that works at the Polynesian. Have you ever run into him?"

She thought for a second and asked, "What group is he in?"

He cocked his head and asked, "Group?"

She almost smacked herself in the forehead. Of course he wasn't going to know what that was.

"Almost every cast member falls into one of five groups,

Deeks, Imports, Defaults, CPs, and Sunsetters.

"A Deek is a Disney Geek. Sadly, I fall in that category. They're the people who moved in, because they love Disney and thought it would be fun to work at Disney World.

"Imports are people from outside the country that Disney imports for added realism. You find a lot of them at Epcot. Most of the kids in the world showcase are imports. Each pavilion is staffed by people from that country.

"Defaults are the sad ones. They are people who don't really want to work for Disney, but have no other choice. Disney is the biggest single-site employer in the U.S. If you can't find a job and you are not a criminal, you can normally fit in somewhere at Disney."

He chimed in, "Oh, like sweeping the pathways."

Sasha paused the game and stared at him.

"You really don't have a clue do you? I pray you don't, for saying something that dumb."

She didn't relent, "When someone applies at Disney, they are tested to see what skills or abilities they have. Disney does their best to put them somewhere they will succeed.

"You didn't talk to anyone who was 'sweeping' did you?"

She could see him squirm a little before he answered meekly, "No."

"Do you know who Disney tends to put into those positions? People with exceptional people skills. For the most part, keeping the paths clean is a cover for what they really do. They are trained to look for people who look lost or are having a bad time and help them out."

He looked at her with a confused look. She could tell he had no idea what she was talking about.

She looked him in the eye and said, "What sets Disney apart isn't what you see, it's what happens to you while you are there. To enhance your experience, or sometimes salvage it, any and all cast members are empowered to do the unexpected.

"For example, two years ago one of those 'Street Sweepers' came across two parents who were trying to console their child. She had an ancient Mickey Mouse doll that was dirty and almost in tatters. The child was crying because the head had fallen off. The cast member could tell the parents didn't have much. They had all the signs of a family trying to save wherever they could. It was obvious that a new souvenir was not in the budget.

"The cast member approached the child and consoled her. She then told the little girl that they had a magic room that fixed and cleaned up old toys. She led the family to the Emporium. She told them to wait as she disappeared behind a door. After a minute she stuck her head out of the door and put on a shocked expression. She looked at the little girl and told her, that not only had her Mickey been fixed but the magic made him grow too. She stepped out of the door with a Mickey almost as big the girl.

"Thankfully, the Emporium has a lot of cameras in it. Someone found the video and passed it around. You wouldn't believe the look on that little girl's face. For the cost of one plush, you better believe Disney made a fan for life."

After a moment she said, "Where was I?"

"You were on 'Defaults.' You still haven't explained what a CP or Sunsetter is," Eric said.

"A CP is someone in the College Program. For the most part, they are all Deeks too. Not too many people enter the College Program just to put it on their resume. The ones that do normally don't last long. The College Program has some fairly strict rules regarding things like curfew and alcohol use.

"Then there are the Sunsetters. They are arguably the best cast members you'll find. The vast majority of them are senior citizens who don't have to work, but do so because they like to stay active and meet new people. I honestly think Disney would be lost without them. It's rare to find people who are happy to go to work."

He looked at her and asked, "You don't like your job?"

She shook her head and said, "I do most of the time. It's just hard when you have to deal with nasty parents or the kids who have never heard the word "no" before. That's why the characters have handlers to help them out. There is also security only seconds away from any character. Some people get too "friendly" or aggressive when they see a character.

"I might be scrappy but when I'm crammed into a massive suit and can only see out of a blurry patch the size of a shoebox, I can't do much to defend myself."

She smiled and then said, "Oh, I forgot to tell you something!"

She saw him perk up before he asked, "What?"

"I'm not done kicking your butt yet!" She quickly started the game again and ran him off the road.

Charting

Jose sat in front of his computer and rubbed his eyes. This was the first serial killer he'd ever been involved with. He'd spent most of the day researching every serial killer he could find. Many aspects fit his case, and he started a list and applied it to the evidence they had.

- The vast majority of serial killers are male.
- Most serial killers seem to share a chromosome abnormality, which explains why they manifest during puberty.
- Serial killers almost never empathize with their victims.
- Friends and family almost never know that someone they know is a serial killer.
- Most abuse alcohol or drugs.
- Most wet the bed.
- Most had no close friends growing up.
- Many act out violent fantasies on animals.
- Most bragged about their killings or left markers behind.

He wasn't sure how this was going to help him. Maybe he could call Victor and see how much background information Disney gathered on their employees. He also figured that could be a waste of time. They wouldn't have DNA records for their employees. Most job applications don't ask about bedwetting.

He took the time to compare the victims. He set up a spreadsheet listing what they knew, and looked for patterns. Every time something popped up, he entered it, even if it seemed frivolous. After an hour of work he had some patterns for all three victims.

- All three victims were boys between 10 and 12 years old.
- They were staying on Bay Lake or the Seven Seas Lagoon.
- They had only been left alone for 15 to 30 minutes.
- They came from unbroken families.
- None of the victims has siblings.
- All the families were affluent.

Jose sat back in frustration. None of that would help. What was he going to do, tell Disney they had to assign security to every 10 to 12 year old boy visiting Disney World? That was beyond foolish. On average, 47,000 people a day visit the Magic Kingdom alone. Unless Disney had a magic wand that could make 10,000 security personnel appear, that wasn't an option.

On the plus side, the third victim finally fit the mold after some research. He was terminally ill and had visited the "Give Kids the World Village." Unlike the other kids at the village, he wasn't staying there and hadn't come to Disney World as a guest of the charity. Instead, his parents had taken him there so he could be with other children who were terminally ill.

He tried to merge everything together. From what he could tell, they were looking for a male who abused alcohol, was a loner, was a cast member, and possibly wet the bed.

He knew drugs wouldn't be involved. Disney tested for that,

so he assumed from what he read that alcohol was involved. The loner part was a decent guess and he wanted the bed wetting part to be true.

The ability to replicate the RFIDs had to point to a cast member. Or did it?

What if they were not looking for a cast member, but someone who was working with a cast member? There were some cases where the serial killer had convinced a spouse to assist.

That idea just made him feel worse. It felt like a step back, and reminded him of just how little evidence they had.

He was so engrossed in his work that he nearly jumped out of his skin when he felt two arms wrap around his bare chest.

"You gonna work all night? You need to get some sleep or else you're in for it tomorrow," Jennica said as she bit his neck.

The thought of tomorrow made Jose groan. Jennica's parents were having a family reunion. For the most part they liked Jose. They would have liked him more if he was Cuban, but at least he was Latino. He often wondered what would have happened if Jennica had shown up with Eric. That idea made him laugh.

"What's so funny," Jennica purred in his ear.

"I was trying to imagine what would happen if you showed

up at a family reunion with Eric, and told everyone he was your new boyfriend."

She burst out laughing and said, "Your buddies on the missing persons side of the fence would end up with a new case."

He didn't doubt it for a minute. Jennica's father reminded him so much of Scarface it wasn't even funny. He had no real reason to believe he was involved in organized crime, but he was willing to bet the farm he knew a lot of people who were.

"Now, don't you forget to be nice tomorrow. You know how my family is."

It took everything he had not to laugh. He certainly knew how her family was. Just like her, one hundred pounds of high velocity explosives. To say her family was emotional was an understatement, but he had to admit, he loved them. When you were with them there was never a dull moment. Being around them was like living life with the volume cranked up to ten.

He certainly needed his sleep tonight. Jose thought about borrowing a detonation suit from the department's bomb squad for tomorrow. He expected a half-ton of explosives to go off when he asked Jennica to marry him in front of her entire family.

Welcome to the Family

Jose stood in the middle of fifty Cubans. Fifty Cubans who had been drinking for over an hour. Fifty Cubans who had progressively gotten louder and louder. He felt like he was in a powder keg. He was starting to think that this was a bad idea.

"You want another drink?" Jennica asked him as she wrapped her arms around neck.

"No, I'm good," he said as he tried to put on a normal smile. He was so nervous he was having a hard time controlling his body language. That meant that he was extremely nervous. He wasn't used to being almost out of control.

She gave him a funny look and whispered in his ear, "I know my family makes you nervous, but at least try to act like you are enjoying yourself."

She pulled away from him and headed for the bar. All he could do was shake his head. He really should have planned this better. He thought he was just going to go down on one knee in front of everyone and ask her. He just couldn't get up the nerve. He needed to find a way to be forced to ask her. He needed someone to force his hand.

He stood there and thought about what to do for a moment. He knew most of the people here would ruin everything if he asked them to help him out. He looked around the yard and realized he only had one option. He needed Jennica's father to help him, but how was he going to broach that subject?

Suddenly it hit him like a sledge hammer. He had to ask Jennica's father for her hand. Why hadn't he thought about that earlier? Knowing her father, he would most likely be expecting him to ask his blessing first. His nervousness may have just saved him from a serious butt-kicking.

He approached Jennica's father and forced himself to make eye contact. The last ten feet were pure torture.

"Could I speak to you in private for one moment, Mr. Lima?" he asked as he put everything he had into not letting his voice shake or crack.

Mr. Lima looked at him for a moment with his normal poker face. He could tell the man was trying to judge what he was up to. Finally, he nodded and motioned for him to follow him into the house.

As he followed Mr. Lima, he couldn't shake the feeling that he was about to walk into the lion's den. They walked through the house and into Mr. Lima's office. He almost stopped in front of the door but managed to force himself through.

Mr. Lima sat behind his desk and motioned for him to take one of the chairs in front of his desk. Not saying a word, Mr. Lima just waited for Jose to explain himself.

He could feel a bead of sweat trickle down his spine. He took a breath to steady himself. There was no turning back now.

"I want to ask for your blessing. I want to ask for Jennica's hand in marriage."

Mr. Lima smiled. He had never seen him simile. He had never seen anything that had unnerved him so much in his life.

Mr. Lima stood up and laughed. He started around the desk and said, "You finally want to make an honest woman out of my daughter? It's about time! I was going to step in soon if you didn't grow a spine."

Jose was so shocked he couldn't respond. He just sat there like a dummy.

"Are you going to stand up or do I have to pull you out of your chair?"

He quickly stood up only to be wrapped in a crushing hug. Mr. Lima was smaller than the average man, but he felt like pure muscle.

"Now. I warn you," Mr. Lima said, as he shoved him back down into his chair.

Mr. Lima took his seat again and the smile disappeared off of his face.

"If you hurt my daughter, I hurt you.

"If you are unfaithful to my daughter, you will find yourself unable to have children.

"If you find yourself unhappy and think you want to divorce my daughter, I suggest you change your name and disappear. If you do not, you will disappear."

Mr. Lima sat there and let what he said sink in for a moment. Jose realized that he was not kidding. Everything he had just been told was all truth, not an exaggeration.

"You now have two options. You can walk away now and never speak to my daughter again, or you can join my family. Which will it be?"

The nervousness he felt melted away. Mr. Lima had always made him nervous because he could never read the man. He never knew where he stood. He knew those days were over. Mr. Lima was making it very clear where he stood.

Jose nodded and said, "Absolutely. Can I call you dad?"

Mr. Lima laughed and said, "You can call me 'idiota,' so long as you treat my daughter right."

Mr. Lima then put his hand up and said, "One more thing. Let me see the ring. I hope you understand, my daughter will not being wearing a cheap ring. If you think she is a cheap woman, we might have a disagreement."

Jose pulled out the small blue box and saw Mr. Lima's eyes light up with recognition.

"I've seen enough. We are now going back outside. The food is being served soon. You will stand next to me. Before the food is served, I will call for everyone's attention. You will ask her then or you will not ask her at all," Mr. Lima said as he leaned forward and smiled.

Eye Opener

Two hours, later Jose found himself sitting in Mr. Lima's office once more. This time, the air was much more relaxed. Everything had gone better than expected. When Mr. Lima called for everyone's attention, Jose hadn't balked at all. He'd called a wide-eyed Jennica over, went down on one knee and proposed.

The chaos that had ensued had been overwhelming. He had barely put the ring on her finger and hugged her when he was pulled away and passed from one crying matron to another. After the women were done, he was pulled off to the side where the men were.

While the women cooed over Jennica and the ring, the men started what seemed to be a never-ending round of toasting. He almost didn't survive. They didn't sip with each toast; everyone was expected to throw back a shot of rum.

To be honest, he more staggered into Mr. Lima's office than walked.

"Well done, son. I can call you that now, because you will be marrying my daughter," Mr. Lima said with a smile.

"We need to have one more drink and discuss a few things."

Jose watched as Mr. Lima opened a crystal decanter, with a dark reddish liquid inside. He poured two measures into ornate glasses and handed one to him.

"This is Legacy by Angostura. Only twenty decanters of this exist. I bought this for an occasion like this. I told myself that I would only share this with the men who were worthy to marry by daughters."

Jose brought the glass to his nose and inhaled the aroma before taking a sip.

"Wow! It's incredibly smooth. I've never had anything like it."

Mr. Lima smiled and said, "I should hope that is the case. It cost over $25,000."

Jose was very thankful he had not been taking a sip when Mr. Lima said that, because he would have spit it out in surprise.

"That is what I think of you, Jose. You have honor. You'd have more honor if you hadn't waited so long, but you finally did the right thing.

"I know you are investigating the Disney World Killer. I might be able to assist you.

"Before I say anything else, I should explain that everything I am about to tell you does not leave this room."

The look Mr. Lima gave him when he said that made his blood run cold, but he was too intrigued to say anything, so he just nodded.

"As you know, Orlando has a small but tight Cuban community. I am one of the leaders of that community. As such, nothing happens within that community without my knowledge. The person you are looking for is not Cuban, and is currently unknown to anyone in the community."

The conviction in Mr. Lima's voice astonished him. How could anyone be so sure?

"How do you know that?" he asked.

Mr. Lima gave him a very serious look and said, "We police ourselves. After the second murder, we did a thorough investigation and asked everyone to stay alert. If the murderer was among us or known to us, there would not have been another murder.

"I know Disney groups everyone as Latino, but we do not. I can provide you with a list of all Disney employees who are Cuban. That should aid you in narrowing your search, but I warn you, do not abuse this information! It is not to be shared with anyone outside the Cuban community."

Jose sat back and tried to digest that. He tried to remember the last time he heard about a Cuban committing a crime in the area. He couldn't think of a single one. He could, however, think of at least half a dozen Cubans who had disappeared without a trace.

He felt the sweat start rolling down his back again.

McKenna

Eric was in a crappy mood. He didn't feel like doing anything, but he was bored out of his mind. He'd already gone over his case notes again and again. There was nothing good on TV and he didn't feel like watching anything on his Amazon Prime list.

Sasha was working late, Jose was at Jennica's family reunion, and it was Matt and Sally's date night.

He was so bored he had even texted Buddy to see what he was doing, only to find out he was working at the Poly.

As a last resort, he decided that he should be a good son for once and call his mom instead of waiting for her to call him like he normally did.

He unlocked his iPhone and selected his mother's home number. It rang a couple of times before a female voice picked up.

It wasn't his mom.

"Hey sis, it's Eric."

"Hey Paddy! I heard about your girlfriend from ma. I can't wait to meet her!" his sister said.

McKenna still lived in Boston with her husband and daughter. She was the reason he didn't feel bad about taking a job in Orlando. He knew his sister was well established in Boston and would be able to help out their mother. It still wasn't easy. He'd only seen his niece a few times, and she was seven years old.

"So ma didn't tell you I'm sleeping with some woman of loose morals, who's going to corrupt me and make me a drug addict?"

"What? What's wrong with you? She only said good things about her. I even looked her up on Facebook and sent her a friend request. I can't remember the last time you had a girlfriend."

"How did you find her on Facebook?" he asked.

"It wasn't very hard. I looked for a cute blonde you were friends with and when I saw ma was friends with her too, it wasn't very hard to figure out."

His stomach bottomed out. His mom friended Sasha? He didn't stand a chance.

"Now Paddy, why haven't you marked her as your girlfriend yet?"

He swallowed and said, "I'm not sure if we are there yet. We've only been out three times."

"Are you seeing anyone else?" McKenna asked.

"No."

"Is she seeing anyone else?"

"I don't think so."

"Then mark her as your girlfriend, numb nuts! Don't wait for her to do it. You think she wants to date a pushover and make all the moves? Grow a pair and go for it!"

He was always amazed how much McKenna was like their father and how much he was like their mother. McKenna was gung-ho and told it like it was. He was more laid back and eloquent.

"Anyways, how's ma doing?" He asked as he tried to change the subject.

"Oh sure, go and change the subject. I'm going to post embarrassing photos of you as a kid on your wall, if you don't mark her as your girlfriend! And ma is fine. She's on a date."

He nearly fell out of his chair.

"She's what?"

"She's out with a guy she met at church. He's a widower. They make a cute couple."

He didn't know why, but he never thought his mother would ever date after his dad died. In the last twenty years he hadn't remembered her dating anyone.

"Wait, why are you at her apartment if she's not around?" he asked trying to turn the table on his sister.

"I'm letting her dog out."

He suddenly felt awful. He didn't even know his mother had a dog. He couldn't remember the last time he checked his mother's Facebook page. He really didn't know anything about what was going on in his mother's or sister's life. How had he gotten so detached? Other people had families that lived hours away and they managed to stay in touch.

"How are things going for you?" he asked with renewed interest.

"Good. Sandra made the honor roll! She reminds me of you in some ways. She's kinda geeky and super smart."

"Gee thanks, sis."

"I meant that in a good way, you goober. Oh, and I better say hi for Andy. He misses having you up here. He said I gave him less crap when you were around."

"Well there is only so much time in a day. If you spoke to me for five minutes that would give him ... five minutes a day of peace and quiet," he said as he tried not to laugh.

"Don't make me come down there! Then again, that might be a good idea. We told Sandra we'd take her this summer. Maybe we can all get together. That would be fun."

He smiled and said, "Yeah, it would be."

"It's been nice talking to you, Paddy, but I have to go pick up dinner. I'll talk to you later."

"Bye sis."

He put his phone down and quickly booted up his Mac. Knowing his sister, he only had an hour to mark Sasha as his girlfriend before the embarrassing photos started showing up.

Running Out of Time

Everyone sat around the table in silence. No one wanted to say a word. They all knew the evidence they had. They had no theories, they had no leads, and they had no hope.

Jose wasn't about to bring up what he had learned from his future father-in-law. Not only would it fall flat in this room, he didn't doubt for a minute that he'd regret it for a very long time.

"Come on guys, we can't give up hope. We're not defeated yet!"

He was stunned. Out of all the people in this room, the last one he expected to fill the role of cheerleader was Dr. Matsuzaka.

Reggie looked up from his coffee and said, "At least some good has come from this. We caught a thieving pedophile. On the down side, the feds took the case since he was involved in a kiddie porn ring that spans most of the U.S."

Reggie thought for a moment and said, "Jose, reach out to your contacts in the press. Give them some info on the pedophile. It's not going help the firestorm we are in for, but it might foster some goodwill in the community."

Jose looked up and said, "I think we need to go full-throttle with the next press conference. No more deflection. We need to admit this is a serial killer and that no one visiting Disney World should leave their children alone at any time."

Reggie nodded and added, "That should get them going, but we need to be careful with what we give away. I say we mention that all the kids were in families where they were the only child, but only if they push us for more info. That seems safe enough without compromising anything."

Dr. Matsuzaka quickly responded, "Yes, but whatever you do, do not mention the murder weapon. If the killer thinks we are looking for it, he could very well discard it."

Reggie nodded and said, "Sounds good. At least we have a plan. Maybe the press will smoke the killer out. Is there anything else?"

Fidel nearly jumped out of his seat and said, "Jose ask marry girl!"

He had only told Eric. How on Earth did El Guapo find out? He suddenly felt the blood drain out of his face. Fidel was Cuban. The community knew. It took less than a day for even El Guapo to find out.

He looked up to see that Reggie was still trying to make out what Fidel was talking about. He quickly said, "Yeah I'm getting married."

Victor sat up in his chair and said, "Congratulations! We needed some good news!"

Eric smiled and chimed in, "Yeah he didn't have to drug her or anything. She willingly said yes!"

That made everyone in the room start laughing.

He didn't even care that it was at his expense. They needed a laugh.

Beer and Buddy

Eric was beyond glad that Jose did the press conferences. Jose excelled at that kind of thing. He knew that if he had to get up there, he'd be nothing more than a liability. Plus, he liked the fact that he could watch the press conferences on TV while he had a beer in his hand.

He took a sip of his beer as Jose took the podium. He knew that Jose needed it more than he did, especially a beer like this one.

He liked scotch, but sometimes you wanted a good beer. He was very picky when it came to beer. He couldn't stand light beers or beers that tasted like Bud. They just didn't have a flavor you could sip and enjoy. Most of those beers were made for chugging, not sipping.

He had developed a taste for low gravity beers, meaning a beer with at least 6.5% alcohol. He found that they normally had intense flavor. They were also hard to find. Most of the supermarkets around here didn't carry them. Thankfully, he'd found a few places in the area that carried single bottle brews.

He liked most of the beers that Unibroue made. In particular Trois Pistoles and Terrible were good one-bottle beers. It was a good thing, too, since they ran around 10 bucks each.

He watched as Jose seemed to flow right through the press conference. Even the questions that came up were not bad. He could tell why, too. Jose had hammered the room with some shocking information. He didn't let them ask if it was a serial killer, he told them flat out. He could tell that had shocked the room.

Within minutes, it was over. He smiled at how well Jose had manipulated the crowd. He decided he was going to get Jose a bottle of Terrible to celebrate.

His phone started going off. He expected it to be Jose or even Reggie calling to get his thoughts on how the conference looked from his end. They often did that.

He was surprised to see that Buddy was calling him.

"Hey Buddy what's up?"

Buddy was a nervous kid, but this time he almost sounded panicked.

"Um ... I just wanted to ask a few questions about a restraining order."

He nearly spit the beer out of his mouth. Why do you need a restraining order? What's going on? Are you ok?"

Buddy managed to stammer back, "Yeah. It's not for me, it's for my sister. She's getting a divorce. She found out her husband has been cheating on her and he's been using and dealing meth."

Eric was never surprised when he heard stories like this one. He'd seen more murders associated with meth than any other drug. Even heroin took a back seat to meth.

Meth seemed to destroy lives faster than anything else he'd seen.

"Friend to friend, this is what you need to do. She needs to pack up her stuff, drive to the police station, fill out the restraining order, and then drive here. I don't care where she lives, she needs to move and move now. Here would be ideal because it sounds like she trusts you, if you are even asking about this."

"Thanks Eric. I didn't know where to turn. I knew you'd know what to do. I really appreciate it. I know she will, too. She didn't deserve this. She's been working full-time and taking classes. She's been trying to make a better life for herself and he was blowing all their money on drugs."

"Buddy, no one deserves that. Do what you can to help your sister. She's going to need someone stable in her life."

"Thanks again. I'll let you know how everything works out."

He shut down his phone and sat back in his chair. He wondered why Buddy's sister had turned to him instead of their parents, but figured he could find out later.

His phone buzzed. He looked at it and a lump formed in this throat. It was a Facebook notification. He was now officially "In a relationship with Sasha Cole."

Different

He almost cried when his phone went off. He snatched it off the nightstand and prayed silently, "*Please, God, no!*"

It didn't work.

"Jose?"

"Eric."

"Please tell me you just wanted to talk to your best friend at 11:30 at night."

"I'll see you at the Boardwalk."

He hung up and seriously considered just staying in bed. What good would it do to get up? He'd been borderline useless so far. What did it matter anymore?

After a moment, he felt anger start to build inside of him. With a grunt he sat up and forced himself out of bed, got dressed, and headed out.

When he arrived at the Boardwalk Inn, Victor greeted him. Eric didn't even have ask, he knew Buddy took the day off to help his sister, plus, he worked at the Poly. The Poly was a Magic Kingdom Resort. This was an Epcot Resort, which bothered him. The killer had a bigger range than they originally thought. Most killers had a comfort zone, which made it easier to hunt them down. Eric had thought that the next target would have been at one of the Magic

Kingdom resorts. Even Fort Wilderness wouldn't have surprised him.

"I hope you're ready. This one is different. I won't say any more, I'll just let you do your thing," Victor said as they started off.

Instead of walking through the main lobby, they headed around the far side of the building. They walked past the white buildings and clean walkways.

"Usually I ask Buddy this stuff, but he's not around. So, I don't get it. What is the theme to this place?"

Victor laughed and told him, "It's the Boardwalk. Like the one in Atlantic City. It would make a lot more sense if I actually took you down to the boardwalk section."

"Any chance we got video footage of the killer this time?"

Victor quickly responded, "It's unlikely considering where the murder took place, but we are looking into it."

He just shook his head. He was used to that response by now. "Any chance there is only one escape route?"

Victor laughed at that and explained, "You wish. They could have come in the way we did, through the main lobby, from the walkway to Epcot, from the walkway to Disney Hollywood Studios or they could have taken the boat that services all the resorts in the area."

Eric grimaced at that. This place was worse than the Magic

Kingdom resorts.

They came to a taped-off area between one of the buildings and a service shed. He was stunned. This was a major break in pattern. That was almost unheard of. Once a serial killer adopted a pattern they normally stuck to it like glue.

He slipped under the tape and greeted Jose and Fidel, before examining the body. It was male child of Asian heritage between 8 and 12 years old. Like the others, his throat was cleanly cut.

He looked around and realized that the killer had most likely lured the child in the small alley, cut his throat and then walked out the back. There were no shoe prints leaving the alley. It would have been impossible to not to track some blood out.

"What's the story Jose? This one doesn't fit the mold."

Jose looked over and told him, "The killer must have been stalking the family. The parents did not leave the kid alone. The kid snuck out. They were staying in a two-bedroom villa. The parents put the kid to bed and then watched TV in their room. They had no idea he was even gone until Victor knocked on their door."

He wondered how Victor knew what room the kid was staying in, but then he noticed the wristband on the victim.

He looked over at Fidel and asked, "El Guapo, any evidence? Looks like the killer had to improvise to pull this one off. Any chance he made a mistake?"

Fidel just shook his head.

This killer was meticulous. Four murders and he had left no solid evidence behind. What kind of a person were they dealing with? To execute so cleanly despite the situation must have taken incredible preparation or shocking intelligence.

He looked up when he heard Jose say, "We can't buy a break. This guy is like some ninja assassin. He seems to just appear out of nowhere, avoids all the cameras and kills without anyone seeing or hearing anything."

Victor gave a sad chuckle and said, "Maybe it's the ghost of Raymond."

He looked at Victor and asked, "Who is Raymond?"

"Raymond was a cast member back in the late '90s. He worked as a custodian. One day he was working on the Skyway when someone accidentally turned the ride on. He got pulled off the tower he was working on. He tried to hold on, but his grip gave out and he fell to his death. After they tore the skyway down, some cast members started claiming that they saw him wandering the parks from time to time."

They were silent for a moment before Jose finally stated, "Well if it's a ghost, that would explain the complete lack of evidence."

Fidel looked confused and asked, "You really think ghost?"

He gave a chuckle and said, "Why not? At this point that seems as feasible as a ninja assassin."

Everyone gave a nervous chuckle, but he could tell some of them were honestly giving the ghost theory a second thought.

Escape

Eric held Sasha's hand as they walked through the Magic Kingdom. Behind him he heard Sally tell Matt how cute of a couple they made. That made him smile. Everything else seemed to be imploding, but he had his friends.

They got on Space Mountain and filled up the entire train. He was in the back with Sasha in front of him. Jose and Jennica were in the middle two seats. Sally was in the front with Matt behind her.

He leaned forward and warned Sasha that Sally was a screamer but she really did like the ride. Sasha must have taken that as some kind of a challenge because she screamed her head off with every turn and dip.

Later he heard someone say "Ice Cream!" Within minutes, each of them had a treat in hand. Sasha grabbed a Mickey Ice Cream bar and accidentally dropped the wrapper. Before he could think to grab it, Sasha bent over and something caught his eye.

"You have a hidden Mickey tramp stamp!" Jennica called out with glee.

Sasha stood up and started to turn red until Jennica said, "I love it! That is so much cuter than mine."

Jennica pulled up the back of her shirt to display her own flowery tattoo.

When Matt saw that he turned to Sally and said, "Maybe you should get a tattoo. I think I'd like that."

Sally responded with a fist to Matt's shoulder and everyone laughed.

Everyone started laughing again a few minutes later when Jose made a lewd comment about Jennica's frozen banana and earned a smack of his own.

Eric hadn't stopped laughing when Sasha asked, with a very serious look, if she had anything on her face. She looked like a toddler with chocolate all over her. She couldn't hold the innocent look, though, and started cracking up.

Everyone went from laughing to roaring when Sasha quickly planted a kiss on his lips, smearing chocolate all over his face in the process.

He needed this. He knew Jose did too. They needed to escape for a while. They had been under so much stress, they were near the cracking point. Hopefully, this would give them the boost they needed to keep going.

They wandered the park for hours, hitting one ride after another. They even all piled together and took photos with every character they came across.

He wished this would never end. He just wanted to stay in this moment with his friends and forget the death he had to deal with on a daily basis.

They finally ended up on Splash Mountain. This time, he was smart and demanded to sit in the back. He wasn't going to get photo bombed or used as a human shield by Matt and Sally again. Plus, he wanted a nice happy photo with Sasha instead of a goofy one.

All of them just sat back and enjoyed the ride. Matt and Sally bobbed their heads back and forth as they sang along. Jose would shield Jennica every time a water cannon went off and sprayed all of them.

They finally came to the final lift hill. He remembered it being dark but this time it seemed almost spooky. He could only see the light at the end of the lift. All he could hear was the loud music and audio track to the ride.

They finally tipped over the top of the hill and plummeted down the chute. This time it was creepy. They had fogged up the bottom of the chute so you couldn't tell where it ended.

He hugged Sasha close and smiled as the ride photo flashes went off. He couldn't wait to see this one.

They hit the bottom of the chute and got drenched. Even in the back, he was soaked.

They exited the ride and headed to the photo area. It took a couple of minutes before their photo popped up.

He looked up at the photo in shock. He and Sasha were sitting happily in the back, but Matt, Sally, Jose, and Jennica were gone. Instead the four victims sat staring at the camera with cold dead eyes.

He couldn't breathe. He turned away from the photo toward his friends. They were gone. The four victims stood in front of him trying to mouth out silent words. He took a step back from them in fear. They reached out for him but he escaped their grasp.

He ran around the corner into the gift shop and bumped into someone dressed all in black. The figure had a hood pulled up, blocking his face. He started to apologize for running into him when the man's hand flashed out, holding a straight razor. Before he could react, he felt the burning of the razor slashing across his throat.

***

Eric bolted upright in bed. He was drenched in sweat and his heart was pounding. After a few seconds, he started to shake and then cry. A feeling of utter hopelessness filled him. It seemed like he was trapped in hell and couldn't escape.

Prep

Eric was rudely awoken only a couple of hours after he managed to get back to sleep. He saw that it wasn't Jose, but Captain Hunter calling him. That was odd.

"Good morning, Captain."

"You need to come down here. We're having a special meeting. Wear a tie. You have one hour."

With that, he heard Reggie hang up the phone. He didn't like this one bit. It was too soon to meet on the most recent murder. Something was up.

He jumped into the shower and just stood there for a while, trying to wash the weariness from his bones. He was dog tired. It felt like he hadn't slept soundly since the murders started. His mind was always running in the background, trying to figure something out. He couldn't shake the feeling that his brain was working on some monster puzzle without his permission.

He shut off the water, dried himself and then sat on the edge of his bed for a moment, as he tried to compose his thoughts. He felt emotionally raw, like anything could make him laugh, cry, or lash out in rage.

He got dressed and tied on his black tie. In a sudden burst of anger, he tore it off of his neck. He wasn't going to wear a black tie. It was too somber. For some reason, he felt that it represented defeat. He was too angry to be defeated so easily. He grabbed his red tie and weaved it into a fat, half Windsor knot.

He looked at himself in the mirror. The red tie was much better. It better represented how he felt.

He knew he had to try to keep a positive outlook. Feeling bad about himself would only serve as a detriment to the case and his friends.

He took a minute to try and think about the positive things in his life. His best friend was getting married and he was the best man. His family was safe in Boston and his niece was on the honor roll. He had a new friend in Buddy, though they made an unlikely pair. Then there was Sasha.

He couldn't help but smile when he thought of Sasha. He was having dinner at her place tonight. He tried not to anticipate anything, but Jose had told him that if he didn't pack his toothbrush and a change of clothes he was a moron.

The thought of all his friends suddenly brought the horror of his nightmare back in full force. The faces were burned into his memory. He couldn't get the children out of his head. They were mouthing something; he couldn't make out what. He took a deep breath and focused on their mouths. If he could only figure out what they were saying, what they were trying to tell him. He tried to slow down the motion. He mentally made their lips move slower.

As his brain registered what they were saying he felt himself go cold and he shivered.

They were saying, "You know …"

The Meeting

Eric walked into the conference room and stopped dead in his tracks. They had a visitor.

He knew the person who sat at the end of the table. He'd never met him, but he'd see him on TV more times than he could count. He now understood why he was told to wear a tie. It wasn't every day you entered a room to see the CEO of a top 100 company staring back at you.

"Do you know who I am?"

He was so overwhelmed he could only nod.

"Please take a seat."

Without saying a word, he sat down and tried not to fidget.

"We want to do everything we can to assist you in finding the killer. To help motivate you I wanted to share some statistics with you.

"Since it was announced that a murderer was stalking families in Walt Disney World, bookings have fallen by 25%. On top of that, we've seen an 80% spike in the number of reservations being canceled. To put that into real life numbers, we've lost millions in expected revenue. When we lose a reservation, we don't just lose the revenue from the room and the tickets. We lose potential food and souvenir sales. There is a huge trickle-down effect.

"Please don't take me as jaded. Overall, the lost revenue is the least of my concerns. Four families have been destroyed in the last two weeks. Countless others have been terrorized. Disney World cannot be a place of terror. It needs to be somewhere people can escape.

"We fully expect the first lawsuits will be filed soon. We will most likely settle them outside of court, but they will still result in enormous losses. With the downturn in attendance and the loss of revenue, we could find ourselves having to cut our workforce.

"We currently employ over 60,000 people here in Florida. It's my goal not to lay off a single one of them, but if we don't stop the killer soon, my hand will be forced.

"The lives of my employees are what concern me the most. I consider them to be part of my family. That's why I am putting up one million dollars, of my own money, as a reward to whoever breaks the case."

It felt like someone sucked the air out of the room. No one moved a muscle or said a word. It seemed to Eric that everyone was trying to figure out if they had just imagined that last statement.

Their guest stood up and said, "I expect daily reports delivered to me directly. I have provided your Captain the necessary information. All of you are free to contact me directly, if it is in any way related to the case."

With that, their visitor left the conference room and another painful silence ensued.

Finally Jose broke the silence, "I guess we know where we stand at least."

Reggie shot him down quickly, "No, we don't. The governor called me this morning. If we do not crack the case in the next twenty-four hours, he's going to ask the Feds for help. You know what that is going to be like. Since there is no evidence of a capital crime, and this is not an interstate crime, they cannot take over the case. That being said, they will get in our way and make our lives a living hell. When we do find the killer they will most likely take the credit. I think it's safe to say none of us want that."

Eric sat back, deflated. He'd never been on a case where the Feds had become involved. He'd heard the stories though, and none of them had been good.

Silence spread across the room. The air was absolutely stifling. Finally Reggie asked, "Anything else?"

Someone had to say something, anything, to lighten the mood. If they left the room feeling this bad about themselves, they might as well all turn in their badges and admit defeat.

"Eric is having 'Dinner' at his girlfriend's apartment tonight for the first time," Jose spouted out.

The shift in the room was shocking. Everyone grabbed at the chance to escape the misery of the case.

"You go, Eric!" Fidel cried out.

Victor patted him on the back and gave him a sly grin.

Captain Hunter looked confused at the reaction until the meaning suddenly hit him. He gave a loud roar of laughter that made Eric blush.

Once Reggie composed himself he said, "Well, that's good news! If you're not feeling up to the challenge, you let me know. I'm more than willing to fill in for you."

Everyone in the room laughed at that crazy remark.

Even Dr. Matsuzaka joined in. She stood up patted him on the shoulder and reminded him not to be selfish. The unexpected comment made Jose laugh so hard, he couldn't talk. The others weren't much better.

Eric took it all in stride. He knew by outing him, Jose had possible just saved the day.

The Call

Jose sat in his office with Eric. They'd been attempting a brainstorming session for over an hour, with few results. Normally when they combined forces they made a lot of progress, but this time nothing was clicking.

He was about to call it quits when the phone rang. He saw the caller ID and almost froze. He quickly looked at Eric and said, "You sit there and no matter what is said you don't say a peep. Don't even breathe, if you can help it!"

Eric gave him a funny look but nodded his acceptance.

Jose answered the phone and put it on speaker.

"Mr. Lima, how are you?"

"I'm fine, Jose. I have someone you need to speak with. Someone who believes they saw the killer last night."

He saw Eric's eyes go wide and he understood why. If this was a serious lead it could be the first break they had gotten in the case.

"How? We questioned everyone at the Boardwalk last night," Jose responded.

"She was not willing to discuss what she saw with the authorities without protection. She is working under a false ID. She is in the country illegally. She keeps a low profile and is terrified of being deported. Speaking to the authorities is not something she does willingly."

He had run into this before. He wished he had spoken to this woman last night. Normally, he could spot the problem and put them at ease. In most cases, he just had to talk about his parents, who had come into the U.S. illegally and the person would let their guard down. It also helped if you spoke to them in their native language. They might know how to speak English, but it wasn't the same. Your first language touched your heart. Nothing else worked as well when trying to get someone to trust you. Thankfully, it sounded like his father-in-law had done the work for him.

"She will have my full protection," he explained.

After a moment a female voice came onto the phone. Her voice trembled when she said hello.

"Good day, senorita," Jose said, trying his best to make his voice sound soft and understanding. It was something he called his priest voice.

"Can you start by telling us what you do at the Boardwalk?"

After a moment the woman said, "I clean. We clean the public areas at night when most of the guests are sleeping.

"I was emptying a trash can near where the body was found. I saw someone dressed oddly."

He hoped this was more than just a wild goose chase. It wasn't sounding good so far.

"What was it that caught your attention?"

"Last night was warmer than usual, for this time of year. It didn't drop below 70. Even people like me who freeze when it's cooler than 60 were not bundled up last night.

"I saw a man bundled up. He had big baggy pants on. He had a big hooded sweatshirt on too, and the hood was up. He looked puffy too, like he had layers on under the sweatshirt. All his clothes were black."

Jose thought for a moment and asked, "Was there anything else that was distinct about the man?"

There was silence for a moment before the witness answered, "He walked funny. He walked like he was stiff."

"How big was he?"

"He was maybe 5'8" to 5'10" it was hard to tell. I couldn't tell if he was fat or thin with all those clothes on."

"Thank you. If I need to talk to you again would you prefer I ask my father-in-law to contact you?"

"Yes, that would be good."

He sat back as he terminated the call.

Eric finally got up the nerve to ask, "What was that about?"

He shook his head, "I'm not sure if you would believe it if I explained it to you."

Eric grinned and said, "Try me."

Jose explained what he had been through a few days earlier when he had proposed to Jennica. He then explained to Eric that he could not repeat what he had just told him, under pain of death.

When he saw Eric laugh he gave him a very serious look and said, "That's not a joke. I'm not saying they are members of organized crime, but I wouldn't mess with them either."

Eric nodded and said, "In some ways I like that. It's like having an asset that isn't restricted by the law. As long as they don't go overboard, I'm all for it. I mean, look at this information we just got from them. It's not much, but it could turn out to be critical. The part about the way the guy walked could be a huge detail. Do you think we should ask Victor to do an inquiry about employees with limps?"

He thought about that for a moment and finally nodded, "I think so. We should ask for an inquiry for male employees, who have limps and do not work the night shift. That might get us some leads to follow."

He sat back and clapped his hands together, "This could be big, Eric! I know it's not much, but finally we might have something."

Eric gave a concerned look and said, "Not to kill the excitement, but let's not put too much hope in this. We could find another dead end. Let's just play it smart and see where it leads us. You also never know what else might fall in our lap from your new network of pseudo spies."

Eric then shook his head and said, "Damn it Jose, why did you wait so long to propose?"

He smiled and wondered the same thing.

Hurricane Sally

Sally charged from one room of her home to another. As she went she cleaned, scrubbed, straightened and organized. No matter how hard she worked, she couldn't relax. Her mind was racing. Something wasn't right, but she couldn't put her finger on it.

Matt had tried to calm her down, to no avail. He'd never been able to calm her down once she was amped up like this. He knew better than to tell her to she was being foolish, too. Every time she got into a tizzy like this, it was for a valid reason.

Sadly, she didn't know what was bothering her. She rarely did, but she always found out in time.

Years ago she got into a tizzy and told Matt something was up. He laughed at her. Twenty minutes later her twin sister called to let her know she was pregnant. Nine months later she told Matt her sister just went into labor. He asked how she knew. She told him she could sense it. He laughed at her. He stopped laughing when he answered the phone five minutes later.

When her grandmother died she had gone into a tizzy without knowing why. The same thing happened again when her grandfather died.

Her tizzies could be good or bad. She almost never knew until after. All she knew was something was going to happen.

Matt jokingly called her tizzies "Hurricane Sally," but even he had become a believer.

"Hey, let's talk this out, and maybe we can figure out what's happening," Matt offered as he forced her to sit down on the sofa.

"Do we know anyone who is pregnant?" he asked.

"Not that I can think of," she responded.

"Do we know anyone who is sick?"

"A few, but none that are very serious."

Matt stopped and changed gears, "Where are your parents?"

"At bingo, like usual."

"Is anyone in our families traveling?"

"Nothing beyond driving short distances."

"Ok, where is Eric?"

"Having dinner with Sasha."

Matt sat back defeated and said, "Let's pray there isn't a car accident, because I can't think of anything else."

That made her nervous. What if someone got into a car

accident? She was up and cleaning again within minutes.

She knew it was more than a feeling. She prayed with all her heart that it was something positive. Then she thought with a smile, maybe Eric would crack his case.

Prep

To say Eric was nervous was an understatement. He'd showered, dressed, soaked his shirt with sweat and showered again. This time, he piled on a ton of talcum powder to combat the nervous sweating. He suddenly realized that he would most likely be taking his shirt off at some point.

He jumped in the shower yet again. This time he decided that he needed to calm himself down. He practiced some breathing exercises to clear his head and calm his nerves. He slowly breathed in and out and felt his heart rate slow.

After he was dressed for the third time, he decided to have a scotch. That would help him calm down. As long as he only had one, it wouldn't be an issue. He spent fifteen minutes trying to pick which one he wanted. He had eight different single malts in his cabinet. They ranged from 10 to 20 years. He finally settled on Speyside. He hadn't tried that in a while. It was a good mid-level scotch that he wasn't afraid to drink on the rocks.

He sat back and closed his eyes. He felt foolish for being so nervous. He blamed it all on his friends. They had made a big deal out of this. It was just dinner.

After a moment, he asked himself why he'd packed his messenger bag if it was just dinner.

After going back and forth for a couple of minutes he realized that he would rather be prepared than not. It was always better to be prepared if you had the chance.

He finished his scotch and looked at his watch. He had to get going soon or he'd be late.

He placed his glass in the sink and headed for the bathroom to brush his teeth.

He got halfway there when his phone buzzed. He prayed it wasn't work. If it was, he considering blowing it off despite the consequences.

He looked down to see it was just Jose wishing him good luck. That just made him nervous all over again. Why did he need luck? He was having dinner with his girlfriend, not betting on the races.

He started brushing his teeth. It took a massive amount of willpower, but he finally relaxed and let his mind wander.

He almost gasped as his mind seemed to explode into action. Suddenly pieces started coming together in unexpected ways. He could see the mouths of the dead children mouthing "You know ..." as one piece fit after another. Details of his walk-through came screaming into his mind followed by bits and pieces of conversations and small details he had ignored. All the crime scenes came flooding into his head.

Everything fit together and in his mind's eye, he could suddenly see the through the killer's eyes. He watched as each crime was committed. He also saw a number of murders that didn't happen because the circumstances were never right.

He dropped his toothbrush and grabbed onto the sink with both hands. The revelation that had just overwhelmed him was so shocking he just stood there for minutes on end. He couldn't move, he couldn't think, he could only stand there in shock.

Finally he managed to stagger over to the toilet and sit down. He put his hands over his face and tried to analyze his revelation for flaws.

After contemplating for a while he decided that he shouldn't act yet. Everything was too fresh in his mind.

He looked down at his watch and realized he was going to be late for dinner. Maybe he'd sort things out in the morning when he had a chance to talk to Jose.

Pizza Time

Sasha nervously did a final run through of her small, beat up home. She had sprayed extra Febreze and shined up the place as best she could.

She had almost bought new sheets, but figured that was dumb. If Eric didn't like her Disney Princess sheets he could go sleep at home. Plus, they were really comfy, for free sheets.

She headed into the kitchen to make sure the pizza wasn't burning. She wasn't a good cook but she could make pizza, and who didn't like pizza? She figured if Eric didn't, that might be a deal breaker, considering it was one of the few things she could cook without setting off the smoke alarm.

She had a big salad laid out too. She found that salad could impress people if you made it really colorful. When people saw all the color they assumed a lot of time went into it. If they stopped and thought about it, they'd realize how easy it was. She really hoped he wouldn't catch that. She wanted to impress him with her ... implied culinary skills.

She looked down at her watch. He was late. That wasn't like him. She really hoped work didn't get in the way. She didn't care if it happened from time to time, just not tonight.

She jumped when she heard a knock at her door. She almost ran across the house. She opened the door and there he stood with a messenger bag slung across his shoulder.

"You are late. The party started already," she said as she cocked her head to the side.

"I could always come back another time," he offered.

She grabbed him and pulled him inside. He gave her a kiss and hugged her close.

She could tell something was wrong. He felt tight, like a spring that was about to explode. Then she realized that he was probably just nervous. That idea made her smile.

"Are you nervous?" she asked, as she gave him a playful smile.

He started to turn red and look nervously around the room.

"Well don't be nervous. Let me get you a glass of wine. I have to take the pizza out, anyway. You do like pizza, right?"

He smiled and said, "Yeah, I love pizza."

She pulled the pizza out of the oven and set it on the cooktop to cool.

"You even have a Disney oven mitt?"

She looked down and laughed before saying, "Yeah a John Carter oven mitt. Someone in corporate must have thought it was going to be the next big thing. Boy, were they ever wrong. They've made a lot of awful decisions when it comes to movies. Think about it. Tron Evolution should have been a big hit, but barely turned a profit. John Carter is one of the biggest busts of all time. Mars Needs Moms was a mega bomb before it. The Lone Ranger was mostly crap and lost a ton of money. Oh, and don't get me started on the Pirates movies."

He gave her a perplexed look and said, "I thought the Pirates movies made a disgusting amount of money?"

She smiled and explained, "Yeah, because people keep going back hoping to see the first one again. The first one was awesome. It hit all the right tones and had a great story. The second one lost 50% of the charm. The third one was easily one of the worst movies I have ever seen. A brain damaged monkey receiving non-stop electric shocks could have written a better script than that."

"I had high hopes for the fourth one only to be seriously disappointed. All but the first movie have too much fantasy crap in them. If I want to see a fantasy movie I'll go see something else. I don't go to a "pirate" movie to watch two hours of lousy fantasy."

He laughed and said, "Maybe Disney should hire you as a consultant to help them avoid crappy movies."

She smiled, turned her nose up and said, "Maybe they should, because someone over there forgot that famous actors and fancy effects are no substitute for a good story."

"I have to use the restroom. Do I have a couple of minutes?" he asked her.

She nodded and said the pizza needed about five minutes to cool.

She followed him into the living room and then plopped down on the sofa. She hoped he wasn't so nervous that his stomach had started bothering him. That could ruin her plans.

Worst Case Scenario

Jose was where he wanted to be: on his porch, with a drink in his hand and his fiancé sitting next to him.

He sat back and closed his eyes. Maybe he'd take a nap before dinner.

His plans were interrupted by his phone. He didn't even look at the caller ID, he just answered it.

"Hello?"

A voice whispered back, "Jose, I need your help."

"Eric? I thought you were supposed to be having dinner at Sasha's? What are you up to?"

"I am at Sasha's. I don't have time to explain. I just need you to listen and record this conversation," Eric whispered back at him.

"Dude, what's your deal, and why are you whispering?"

"Jose! Shut up and listen, damn it! Start recording and listen!"

He just rolled his eyes and started recording the call.

"Fine, but you better have a real good reason for this. I'm not in the mood for games."

He listened as some rustling came through the earpiece of his phone. He figured Eric had just put the phone in his pocket. This better not be some sick joke. If he was about to get noisy with Sasha he was hanging up.

He heard Eric open a squeaky door and take a few steps. What he heard next made his blood run cold.

He heard Eric ask, "Why do you have a straight razor?"

Eric hadn't even finished the sentence before Jose exploded into motion. His drink crashed to the porch and shattered. Jennica called out in surprise and asked what was wrong with him.

What she said didn't even register with him. He was already at a full run and heading toward his car.

He had just made the car when he heard Sasha reply, "I use it to shave my legs."

He had managed to turn the car over and slam it into gear by the time he heard Eric respond, "No. You use the razor on the side of your tub for that."

As he peeled out of his driveway his Bluetooth took over just in time for him to hear Eric cry out, "Sasha wait!" followed by the unmistakable sound of two gunshots.

The Scene

Jose had his siren blaring and the lights going in his unmarked Dodge Charger. The engine roared as he weaved in and out of traffic. He had to get to Sasha's house before it was too late.

He didn't dare call in the crime yet. The last thing he wanted to do was spook Sasha. For Eric's sake, he had to take her by surprise.

He slowed down as he pulled onto her street. Screeching tires was not the most inconspicuous way to arrive at someone's house when you were trying to take them by surprise.

He quickly called officer down, all units respond, and the address as he pulled up in front of the house.

He jumped out of the car, but didn't shut the door. The noise could give him away. He approached the door and took a breath. He had to hit hard and fast and hope she wasn't holding the gun since he hadn't had time to grab his own.

With a swift, powerful kick, he blew the door off its hinges.

He saw Sasha on her knees wiping blood off the floor. Five feet to her right, a handgun sat on a side table. He was fifteen feet from the gun.

They locked eyes and no one moved for a moment. They

both erupted into motion at the same time. She easily made it to the gun first.

He knew he didn't have a chance to grab the gun before Sasha could get to it, so he had moved so he could intercept her instead. He knew that getting to a gun was not as important as being able to use it. He knew Sasha didn't have time to aim and fire.

He was moving at full speed when he dropped to his back and went into a slide on the smooth, tiled floor. He pulled his knees up to his chest and curled his spine.

Sasha had just started to turn the gun his way when he reached her. All he had was momentum and the power stored in his body. With all his strength, he snapped out his legs and arched his spine. The effect was devastating.

His feet connected solidly with Sasha's chest. The impact caused her head to snap forward violently and her arms to fly out like a rag dolls.

The impact was so violent, her hundred pound frame flew across the room and crashed into the wall, where she crumpled and remained motionless.

When he stood up, he was shaking so badly he could barely tear the window treatments off the wall and tie her up with them.

Confession

Jose and Fidel stood at the one way window looking into the interrogation room. He'd hoped that making Sasha wait would have upset her. He was wrong. If she was upset in the least, she didn't show it.

Reggie joined him and barked out, "You go in there and you break that bitch! Take Fidel with you. He'll have to fill in for Eric."

He nodded and said with a voice that could cut steel, "Gladly. Let's go, El Guapo."

To his credit, the normally jolly-looking Fidel now looked like 200 pounds of uncontrollable fury. At first, he thought it was just a show, but then he paid close attention to his body language. He'd never seen the man so angry.

He sat down with a pile of papers and folders in front of him. He looked at Sasha and said, "We have you on assaulting a police officer and attempted murder. If Detective Highland doesn't make it through surgery, that charge will be upgraded to murder."

To his surprise, a very concerned look came over her face. It seemed like she hadn't wanted to kill him or even hurt him. She had panicked.

"Our forensic expert is matching your razor to the victims now. I don't doubt for a moment it is going to be a match."

He pushed a list of dates, times, and locations toward her and said with an icy voice, "Why don't you tell me where you were during the times listed. Let's start with that first one. The one at the Poly. What where you doing then?"

He had run into a lot of hardened criminals in his time, but nothing had prepared him for her response.

Without any change in composure she simply said, "Killing a black boy."

An hour later, he and Fidel sat in Captain Hunter's office. By the end, he was so blown away by the details Sasha had freely admitted to, that Fidel had to chime in to keep the information flowing.

Disturbing wasn't even the word to describe what he and Fidel had just gone through.

"She confessed to everything?" Reggie said in disbelief.

He was so drained, he couldn't even muster an answer. Fidel had to answer for him, "Yes sir. She confess to all."

"How did she pull it off?"

He rubbed his eyes and explained, "Because of her job as Mickey Mouse, she had access to the entire RFID system. She had to have some access to sync and test her costume, but why or how she was allowed access to everything is beyond me. It was that access that allowed her to replicate the wrist bands.

"She'd spent time checking out all of the resorts well before she started killing. She knew them inside and out. To aid in not being noticed, she looked different every time. She always dressed as a man, though. She even had large platform shoes to make her look much taller.

"I have to warn you that this next part might disturb you. She only killed four kids, but had stalked no fewer than fifteen families. She was extremely meticulous. If the situation did not meet her requirements, she walked away."

At hearing that, Reggie pulled out three glasses and poured a large measure of Old Crow into each one. He normally couldn't stand the swill, but tonight he gladly took his share.

After taking a big pull off his glass, Reggie couldn't help but ask, "Why? What kind of a monster could do this?"

"Sir, I'm not convinced she is a monster; disturbed yes, but a monster no. By the age of eight, she had lost everyone who loved her. She was alone and in the custody of the state. She ended up at a boarding school where she was molested by a group of rich, blue blood, kids for several years. It's too bad her juvenile records were sealed. According to her, she acted out and put a couple of them in the hospital. She didn't mention anything else, but I'd bet the farm there is a lot more violence in her background. She freely admitted that she wasn't trying to defend herself when she put those kids in the hospital. She was trying to inflict maximum damage. She would have beaten them to death if no one had intervened. She said she felt a high unlike anything she had ever experienced after. As you know, that is a startling fact."

Reggie nodded and said, "People who thrive on violence only escalate over time. Sounds like she graduated to murder."

Fidel piped up and added, "She only kill rich kids who act like … dicks?"

Fidel looked at him for confirmation. He nodded and confirmed, "I don't think I could have put it better myself, El Guapo. She targeted the rotten spoiled brats she came in contact with. She knew they were rich based on the hotel they were staying at, and how the kids and parents were dressed. She only focused on boys in some kind of sick revenge ploy. In her head, she thought she was doing the world a favor."

Reggie finished his glass and asked, "How did Eric know?"

He shook his head, "I don't know. He was dating her, but I don't think he knew until tonight."

Reggie just shook his head and said, "I don't care how he did it but he did." Before he could continue his voice cracked. "I just hope we get the chance to ask him."

Tears started to fall down Reggie's checks. Everyone soon joined him.

Reggie wiped his eyes and firmly said, "We have to keep the fact that Eric was dating her under wraps. If that somehow got out to the media, we'd be hung out to dry.

Granted it broke the case for us, but the media won't see it that way."

Jose slowly nodded his head in agreement. They were going to have to bottle up a number of facts about this case.

Epilogue

Jose walked into the hospital room in a somber mood. On one side of the room sat the geeky, redheaded kid he'd met at the Wilderness Lodge. On the other side, the gentle giant Matt had managed to cram his frame into a small chair. Right next to the bed was a red-eyed Sally. She was sitting silently, holding Eric's hand.

Eric had a tube in his stomach and another one in his chest. Both arms had IVs in them. On a positive note, he didn't have a breathing tube in. That was a very good sign, but overall, he looked very pale and more dead than alive.

Before he could ask, Sally quietly whispered, "He's sleeping. He's really drugged up and in a lot of pain. It hurts for him to talk. Before he fell asleep he wrote this down in case you visited."

Sally handed him a notebook.

He opened it and was stunned by the information inside. It was a huge list of all the items that Eric had pieced together. He truly had cracked the case wide open. Some of the details Eric had picked up on would have blown right by Jose. The kid's mind was like an iron trap. He'd remembered small things, like a comment Sasha had made during dinner. She had apparently known where the bodies were found in the rooms. That was something they hadn't released to the public.

As he went through the list, it astonished him. Eric had

nailed the connection between the victims and Sasha simply based on some seemingly flippant comments she had made over the course of two weeks. He'd also nailed how she selected the victims and alluded to the fact that it was likely she had followed many more victims without success. He had figured out almost every single aspect of the case without a confession.

"Sasha?"

He looked up to see his friend was awake. He knew what his friend wanted to know. He could tell that despite what he had figured out, and despite being shot, Eric desperately hoped he was wrong.

It took every ounce of strength he had to muster the words.

"She confessed to everything. She killed all of them."

Despite the pain, his friend started to sob uncontrollably. Jose felt tears welling up in his eyes. He knew Eric's physical wounds would heal. He just prayed that someday the emotional ones would, too.

Other Books by A. Antonio

The DW Mysteries

"World" Killer
Around the "World"
Imagineered Death

The Advocates

Nemesis
The Shoals
Sojourn

The Unity

Titan One
The Harvesters
Changeling

The Woman in White (No ETA)

Fair Weather
Beast
Camden Lock

A. Antonio is an unsigned, independent author.

For more information please visit:

http://thecousinmickeydoesnttalkabout.blogspot.com/